'Amy, are you sure you're all right?'

Max took her arm as they reached the door.

Gently Amy shook herself free from his hand and the electric pulses that his touch was sending along her nervous system. She knew she must ignore the concern in his grey eyes and the tone of his voice, must not read anything more into them. 'I'm fine.' She was pleased with her firm voice. 'I just can't wait to get stuck into my work.'

Dear Reader,

Practice Nurse Amy Kincaid finds that she is IN SAFE HANDS in Margaret O'Neill's latest GP story, while Canadian physiotherapist Jane Easter tries to convince Dirk that the unknown can exist in Sara Burton's BEYOND HEAVEN AND EARTH. A convalescent home is the unusual setting for Clare Lavenham's offering in SISTER AT HILLSIDE, and the beautiful Great Barrier Reef is the backdrop for Judith Worthy's STORM IN PARADISE.

Travel the world without leaving home!

The Editor

Margaret O'Neill started scribbling at four and began nursing at twenty. She contracted TB, and when recovered, did her British Tuberculosis Association nursing training before general training at the Royal Portsmouth Hospital. She married, had two children, and, with her late husband, she owned and managed several nursing homes. Now retired and living in Sussex, she still has many nursing contacts. Her husband would have been delighted to see her books in print.

Recent titles by the same author:

DOCTOR ON SKYE
A QUESTION OF HONOUR

IN SAFE HANDS

BY

MARGARET O'NEILL

MILLS & BOON LIMITED
ETON HOUSE   18–24 PARADISE ROAD
RICHMOND   SURREY   TW9 1SR

First published in Great Britain 1992
by Mills & Boon Limited

© Margaret O'Neill 1992

Australian copyright 1992
Philippine copyright 1992
This edition 1992

ISBN 0 263 77919 X

Set in 10 on 11½ pt Linotron Baskerville
03-9211-55275

Typeset in Great Britain by Centracet, Cambridge
Made and printed in Great Britain

CHAPTER ONE

CASTLEMINSTER MEDICAL CENTRE was large—four separate general practices and several alternative medicine practitioners under one roof, newly installed in three elegant Queen Anne houses carefully interconnected, near the Cathedral in the centre of the town. There was a lift to all floors, thick forest-green carpets in the consulting-rooms and corridors, a few cheerful flower studies on the pale walls, and *up-to-date* magazines in the waiting-rooms. The children's waiting area contained toys, books and a small television providing suitable videos.

The reception staff monitored the comings and goings of patients on TV screens and ushered them to and fro, by an audio system, or on a personal escort level if this was necessary. There were well equipped examination and treatment-rooms, and solid X-ray rooms in the basement, so that much could be done for patients on the premises. It was planned that minor operations would be carried out in the near future. Private and National Health patients were all seen by appointment.

It was the collective brainchild of senior members of several local practices, who had been working on an idea to improve the medical services for their patients. 'There's never enough money about for anyone to benefit from all the new advances in medicine,' one elderly practitioner had observed. 'If we're to protect our patients, we must make ourselves as efficient as possible and fight lack of money by working together. Our future lies in group effort and sharing of facilities.

We'll pool all our resources and expertise; those of us who have specialities will put them at the disposal of our colleagues, so cutting down on hospital appointments and so on. We'll buy drugs in bulk and make better use of ancillary staff, and share the expense of electricity, small business rates, and so on.'

Out of this pronouncement had arisen the Castleminster Medical Centre, St Anne's House.

Amy Kincaid joined the centre as a part-time assistant to the centre manager three weeks after Castleminster had begun to function, and a week after she had moved to the village of Monkton, a few miles out of town.

'Nurse,' said Janet Brown, the centre manager, on the third day that Amy Kincaid was on duty, 'will you please take Dr Bentley's chest clinic this afternoon?'

It was, of course, an order, not a request, however politely it had been phrased. Amy felt a small twinge of anxiety, and was immediately ashamed of her reaction. She had not as yet met this particular doctor. He had the reputation for being rather austere and remote, and some said even unfriendly towards the staff. Well, she assured herself, there was nothing for her to be concerned about. She was a good nurse, and as long as he was a good doctor they would get along fine on a professional level. At the end of the day, this was what was important.

None of the staff, medical or nursing, knew Dr Bentley well. He had only recently joined one of the practices in St Anne's House. His reputation for being a cold individual was, therefore, a rather hastily formed opinion. 'Very clever,' somebody had told Amy when she first arrived. 'And snooty with it!'

Well, thought Amy that afternoon, preparing the

examination-room in readiness for Dr Bentley's clinic, I'm going to give him the benefit of the doubt, and wait and see how things turn out. Who knows, he might be all sweetness and light. She giggled at the very idea of the man being so at variance with his reputation.

'Glad to see you find your work amusing,' said a deep voice, steely with irony, from the doorway.

Amy took a deep breath before turning round to confront the doctor, for she had no doubt that it was he who had spoken. A grey man, was her first impression. A lean, distinguished grey man, she amended, his black hair heavily streaked with grey, luminous grey eyes topped by strongly defined black brows, a clever long face, long straight nose, and a wide well-marked mouth, which looked somehow vulnerable in such chiselled, handsome features. Broad shoulders clothed in expensive grey suiting, a pristine white silk shirt, and a grey silk tie with a tiny darker grey motif.

Amazing, she thought, he's a kind man. No one could have such a tender mouth as that and not be kind. In answer to his comment, she said with all the composure she could muster, 'A private joke, Doctor, not worth repeating.'

He muttered something that sounded like 'Hmph,' and then to her surprise stepped forward, offered his hand, and introduced himself.

'Max Bentley,' he said in a velvet voice that she guessed must seduce his patients to a suitably receptive state. 'And you are——?'

'Amy Kincaid, staff nurse, new, and therefore unfamiliar with your clinic, but competent, I believe.'

'I'm sure you are, Staff. I'm pretty new, too, to this set-up. I've only just joined Dr Makepeace and Dr Hool in the practice.'

'Yes, so I understand.' Amy felt a bit at a loss. The

iron man whom she had expected had turned out to be, if not exactly a pussycat, then a softer, more approachable person than she'd been led to believe. Remembering her thoughts about him proving to be all sweetness and light, she found herself smiling without meaning to do so. She had already decided that he certainly wasn't a pussycat—he had claws, even if they were kept sheathed—but near enough to make her earlier prognostications valid.

'Another joke not for the telling?' asked Max Bentley.

'I'm afraid so,' she said, giving him a nice smile, which he interpreted as ravishing.

What a stunner! he was thinking to himself, admiring her tawny fair hair, cut short, almost cropped, and yet looking utterly feminine. The almond-green eyes, slightly slanted, gave a vaguely Oriental look to her heart-shaped face. She had short smudges of dark blonde eyebrows and long golden-brown eyelashes, which swept down demurely on to high cheekbones when she was concealing her thoughts beneath half-closed lids. She had, too, the neatest of retroussé noses. She was totally and quite unexpectedly fascinating. He was determined not to fall victim to her charms. No way was he going to be seduced by another blonde beauty—once was enough.

He pulled himself together and said briskly, 'Well, in that case, we'd better get on with our work, hadn't we?'

Amy was a bit startled by his change of tone, but relieved in a way. She was pleased to find that the formidable Dr Bentley was not so formidable, and she was quite happy to have simply a good working relationship with him, with no overtones of anything more intimate. Quite apart from having enough to occupy her at home, she had had, at least temporarily, enough of close friendships with men.

The medical notes were all on disk, though, because they had only recently been computer filed, the old handwritten notes in buff envelopes were also in use. Amy had already placed the notes on the desk and flicked up the relevant disk on the screen, relating to the first patient.

'Mr Norris Black,' she said. 'Shall I bring him in?'

'Please—and help him off with his clothes, Nurse— the poor old boy's arthritic as well as bronchitic.'

Mr Norris was eighty-two, breathless, bent and seeming a little confused. His wife, only a few years younger, but much sprightlier and more on the ball, was with him.

'Shall I come in too, Nurse?' she asked. ''E gets a bit muddled at times.'

'I think perhaps Dr Bentley would rather see him alone at first,' Amy told her. 'Even if he can't answer all his questions, it sometimes gives the doctor quite a lot of information, knowing what the patient is capable of himself.'

Mrs Black bridled slightly. 'Well, just as you say, Nurse, but I'm 'ere if needed.'

Soothingly Amy reassured her, 'Dr Bentley will certainly want to see you after he's examined Mr Black. He knows how important you are to your husband's wellbeing.'

Mrs Black was somewhat mollified. She gave Amy a faint smile. 'All right, I'll wait, then.' She settled herself in the comfortable armchair in the waiting area outside the clinic-room, her vast handbag clasped tightly on her lap.

That Max Bentley was a kind and considerate doctor became clear within a few minutes of the patient entering the room. He helped Amy divest Norris Black of his many layers of clothing, readjusted the examination couch so that the old gentleman could be reasonably comfortable while he was being examined, and reassured him constantly. Like all the best doctors that she had worked with, he explained to his patient what he was doing, and why, ignoring the fact that Mr Black was rather deaf and, so they had been informed, partially confused.

He listened intently to the wheezing, whistling breathing through his stethoscope, moving the head of the scope gently over the white, barrel-shaped chest. He paid a great deal of attention to the bases of both lungs, and asked the patient to cough.

'Eh?' said the old man.

Max Bentley patted his thin shoulder reassuringly, and spoke very plainly. 'Cough, please, Mr Black.' He suited action to words, pretending to cough vigorously.

'Oh, cawf,' said Mr Black. 'I can do that all right, and bring up a lottov stuff from me chest.'

'Good—spit it out in this, old chap.' Max held out a hand for the sputum carton that he seemed to know Amy would have at the ready. 'Now,' he said, 'cough and spit.'

Amy supported Mr Black in a sitting position while Max Bentley held the carton in position. He grinned at Amy over the patient's head. 'I thought we'd have a hell of a job getting him to do this,' he said quietly. 'I was going to leave it for you to do later.'

'I dare say I would have managed,' Amy said, trying to sound cool and professional, but finding herself smiling back, won over by the doctor's cheerfulness and assistance with what was, after all, her job.

It took a while to get Mr Black back into his clothes, while Dr Bentley filled in the details of his examination on the computer file.

Mr Black was intrigued to see the doctor sitting at the keyboard tapping out the information.

'What's all this new-fangled stuff?' he asked in the loud voice of a deaf person.

Amy explained that it was his medical notes. To her surprise, he seemed to understand. He gave a hoarse, crackly laugh. 'Don't suppose I can look at them any more 'an I could the old 'uns,' he said, casting a sly look in the doctor's direction.

Dr Bentley raised his head. 'Why not? They're your notes, Mr Black.' He waved a beckoning hand. 'Come on, come and have a look—you're welcome.' He spoke to Amy. 'Nurse, would you please ask Mrs Black to come in, and we'll have a chat about her husband's condition.'

Mr Black settled himself in the chair that the doctor had offered him and stared at the screen. 'Well, I'm blowed!' he said. 'Have I got all that wrong with me? This bronch- something, and what's this?' He leaned forward and stared hard at the screen, lifting his spectacles up and down with jerky movements of his arthritic hands, in an attempt to focus them. 'Pleu-ro—no, it beats me. What is it, Doc?'

'Pleurodynia, Mr Black, that's where a lot of your pain comes from in your chest. It's caused by rheumatism in the muscles of the chest wall.'

'And I've really got all those fancy things wrong with me?'

'Afraid so,' replied Max, producing a warm smile to take the sting from his words. 'But we can do a lot with medication these days—make you more comfortable, help you enjoy your food more, that sort of thing. Can't give you a cure, unfortunately, but certainly we can make life more bearable.'

'Well, that'd be something,' said the old man, who

had been watching the doctor's lips intently as he was speaking. 'In fact, that's all I want really. Make life a bit easier for the missus. It ain't much fun for her, having ter look after an old crock like me.'

At that moment Amy ushered Mrs Black into the examination-room.

''Ere!' she began in an angry and frightened voice, seeing her husband sitting beside Max in front of the computer screen. 'Wot you doin', Norris, worrying the doctor like this?' She looked as if she might pull her husband from the chair by force. 'I'm sorry, Doctor, truly I am. That's why I wanted to come in with 'im. 'E seems to have lost all sense of what's right and wrong, the silly old thing.' Her tone was half affectionate, half irritable.

'It's all right, Mrs Black, I asked your husband over to look at his files. We were discussing his diagnosis and treatment.'

Mrs Black gaped. 'Look 'ere,' she said, 'you're not 'avin' me on, are you, as if 'e knows wot's wot?'

'No, of course not, Mrs Black. Your husband can understand what's going on.' Max turned to the old man. 'Isn't that right?' he asked.

Mr Black nodded, though he looked rather apprehensively at his wife.

Max continued, 'Your husband has got suddenly very deaf, Mrs Black, and his eyes aren't too good. He needs testing for new specs. He doesn't hear much that's said to him, even with his hearing aid. That needs checking too, and he can't see what people are saying unless he's very close to them, so people think he's confused. He isn't, no more than you or I. He just makes a stab at understanding what's said and gets tired trying to lip-read. This in turn makes him lose concentration and makes him appear even less able.'

Amy had the feeling that, had it been anyone but Dr Max Bentley who had said these things, Mrs Black would have ignored the suggestion completely, and probably walked out in high dudgeon. As it was, she just sat looking at the doctor in stunned silence, before turning to look at her husband with a curious mixture of relief and disbelief on her bright, almost girlish face.

'Is that true, Norris, wot the doctor says—are you more deaf than daft?'

Mr Black said, 'Eh, what's that, Dolly?'

Both Max and Amy smiled sympathetically at the two elderly people. Max said, 'You'll have to practise speaking very plainly, Mrs Black, and facing your husband, at least until he has a better hearing aid. This one's a bit ancient.'

'Can he get another one, then?'

'Oh, yes, I'll give you a note to take to the hospital to see a specialist and they'll fix him up. As to seeing an optician, there are plenty in the town. I'm sure you can make an appointment to see one.'

'Well, we'll 'ave to see about that, but I expect we'll manage soon.'

'Of course there's a charge now for an examination, but you can recover the cost, Mrs Black. There are ways that you can claim back the charge.'

'We don't want charity, Doctor, only wot we're entitled to. We'll manage.'

'But the point is, Mrs Black, your husband *is* entitled to a free examination. We'll have our own optician here from next week. On your way out, see the receptionist and tell her I want Mr Black to have an appointment as soon as possible. We'll get your husband fixed up with new specs and a new hearing aid, and life will be vastly improved for both of you.'

'Ain't 'e nice?' said Mrs Black loudly, as Amy escorted her and her husband through the door.

'Yes, very nice,' conceded Amy. She dared not look in the doctor's direction. He must have heard the compliment, and was probably embarrassed.

She was surprised by his patience. Clearly he cared much for his patients. Her heart warmed to the enigmatic doctor with his reputation for coldness.

She wondered who had first been responsible for this assessment, and guessed it might be a member of staff who'd hoped to make it on a personal level, and failed. In that they were probably right. Dr Max Bentley was all that might be desired as a medical practitioner, but he was almost certainly cool and detached where personal relationships were concerned.

There was no doubt about this being the case when the chest clinic came to an end. The doctor had seen ten patients in all. All of them were meticulously examined and their condition discussed in depth. They were either patients whom he had seen before or referrals from the other doctors in the practice. Only at the end of the session, when Amy was filing disks and handwritten notes, to be kept until duplicate disks were made, did she realise that three of the patients were on the private list. No way, from Dr Bentley's manner or procedures, could she have guessed at their identity. Her admiration for the man and the doctor rose dramatically.

He left just before she did, wishing her a cool, 'Goodnight,' as he let himself out into the corridor. But a moment later he pushed open the door again and gave her a smile of such warmth that she blinked. He thanked her for her help. 'Sorry I have to leave you to clear up,' he said in the velvet voice he had used when he introduced himself, 'but I have to rush away.'

Amy found her voice. 'That's perfectly all right, Doctor. It's my job anyway.' She returned his smile and continued stacking instruments in the steriliser.

'Well, goodnight once again, and many thanks.'

The corridor was too well carpeted for her to hear his footsteps, but she could imagine his long, measured stride taking him purposefully down to the car park. Where, she wondered, was he rushing to, and to whom was he rushing? If any of the rumours about him were true, he had no wife to go home to, so his most likely assignation would be with a beautiful, sophisticated woman, as lean and elegant as himself.

Amy looked down at her own well-rounded figure with her nose wrinkled in contempt. She wasn't fat, but she could certainly do with losing a few pounds.

Forty minutes after the clinic finished, Amy drove back to the village of Monkton, a few miles from the cathedral city of Castleminster. She was tired but happy after a busy day. Her session in the chest clinic had been rewarding. No matter what her nursing colleagues might say, she had found Dr Bentley easy to work with.

True, he had left as soon as his clinic was over, with a cool, 'Goodnight,' though he had come back to thank her for her help. His smile had been friendly, but he had remained polite and distant. He had not stayed to discuss any of the patients he had seen or asked for her reaction to them or to the work. And although she would have welcomed such intercourse, Amy was satisfied with the way the clinic had gone, and with the doctor's and her own performance there.

Her little car, a nearly clapped-out Fiat of the smallest variety, huffed and puffed its way home, grinding noisily up the hills, but sailing blissfully down, grateful no doubt to be relieved of changing gears.

She picked up Jennifer from the little mixed prepara-
tory school that she attended in the village. Arrangements had been made for Jenny to stay at school and
have her tea with the boarders, until collected.

Jenny, a small, bright replica of Amy, bounced into
the car, and in the few minutes that it took them to
drive home, gave Amy a breakdown of what had
happened in school that day.

'I've been put in charge of Rose,' she said. 'Rose is
new to the school too, like me, but she's shy, and she
can't hear very well.'

'Do you mean she's deaf?' asked Amy.

'Well, almost. She wears a thing in her ear to help
her, but it doesn't seem to work always, and Mrs
Campion says I must help her. You know, if she doesn't
hear something in the lesson, or wants to leave the room
and is afraid to put up her hand.'

Amy frowned. 'Isn't that going to stop you getting on
with your own work?'

'Oh, no, the work's easy. They're ever so much more
behind here than at my other school. Anyway, I like
Rose, she's pretty and nice, just like her name.'

A rose by any other name, thought Amy, deciding
not to make an issue about schoolwork, but making a
resolution to speak to Mrs Campion about the matter.
It was a bit disquieting to find that Jenny was so
confident about her lessons. Did it mean that Campion's
School, which had a reputation for high standards as
well as kindly owner-teachers Mr and Mrs Campion,
was not so academically advanced? Jenny was a bright
girl, but was she really so ahead that she could afford to
be almost complacent?

Not for the first time in the last few years, Amy
wished there were someone in whom she might confide,
discuss her problems, especially the problems which

seemed never-ending in connection with her other sister, Belinda.

Who, she thought, would want to be responsible for a teenager these days? The gulf that existed between her twenty-five years and Belinda's eighteen seemed impossible, at times, to cross.

She gave herself a mental shake as she and Jenny got out of the car. 'What shall we have for supper?' she asked.

'Baked beans on toast,' said Jenny predictably.

'OK, but fresh fruit to follow,' agreed Amy.

CHAPTER TWO

JENNY raced upstairs to change out of her school uniform as soon as they got home. The winter uniform at Campion's was a green and red tartan skirt for the girls, and similarly patterned trousers for the boys, white shirts, tartan ties and grey pullovers. The Campions had both Scottish and Irish connections. When Jenny came down, she was wearing jeans and a pale green jumper. It matched her eyes, just as it would have matched Amy's.

While Amy was getting supper ready, Jenny sat at the kitchen table doing her homework. What a lovely girl she is, thought Amy, so cheerful and loving. She sighed, wishing the same could be said of Belinda, but knowing it was wishful thinking.

Belinda, even as a small girl, had never been happy or contented. She had always grumbled, always blamed Amy or anyone else who was around if anything went wrong, but so innocently, so prettily, that even their mother usually believed her version of events. And men, including Father, were as putty in her hands.

Occasionally Belinda was found out in her deception, but when she was she seemed to have the power, the charm, to overwhelm any opposition, especially if the opposition was male. Even Amy, who probably knew her better than anyone, was sometimes cajoled into believing her sister had been wronged.

The phone in the hall rang just as Amy and Jenny heard Belinda's key in the lock.

'It's all right,' she called, 'it's probably for me, I'll take it.'

Amy pushed the kitchen door closed.

'I bet it's another boyfriend,' said Jenny in a resigned voice. 'I think all she does at college is collect boyfriends.'

Amy was determined to be understanding. 'Well, you're only young once,' she said. 'She's got to have a bit of fun.'

'You don't get much fun, do you?' said Jenny with the sublime innocence and acuteness of her eight years. 'You haven't had fun for a long time, not since before Mummy was ill and died.'

Her pretty little mouth trembled, and Amy flung down the spoon with which she was stirring the beans and went quickly to the small girl's side. She gave her a great hug.

'Oh, Jenny, looking after you is fun, and now that I've got this smashing job, which I'm enjoying as much as you're enjoying your new school, we're going to have a lovely time.

Belinda flung the door open. 'It's for you,' she said to Amy. 'A bloke with an absolutely smashing voice!'

'For me?' echoed Amy.

'That's what I said—well, actually he asked for Mrs Kincaid, but I said he'd better speak to you.'

Jenny asked in a trembling voice, 'Did he mean Mummy? But Mummy's dead, he couldn't mean Mummy.'

Belinda looked a bit uncomfortable. She was fond of her small sister in a rather detached fashion. 'Well, he wouldn't know that, Jen, would he?' She stood looking pretty and helpless and big-eyed at the other two girls. 'Sorry,' she muttered as Jenny burst into tears.

'Oh, Belinda!' snapped Amy furiously. 'It couldn't

have been a worse time to mention. . .we were just
talking about Mummy.'

Belinda tossed her tangle of bright hair away from
her face, her violet-blue eyes hard. 'Well, I didn't know,
did I? Look, I'm sorry about Jen, I know she still misses
Mummy, so do I, but we've got to get over it some time,
haven't we, and he did ask for Mrs Kincaid.'

Amy hugged Jenny again. 'Look, love, I'd better
answer the phone. I won't be a minute—will you be all
right?'

'Yes,' sobbed Jenny.

Amy turned to Belinda. 'For goodness' sake give
Jenny a cuddle,' she said as she hurried out into the
minute hall and picked up the receiver.

'Yes?' she asked briskly, taut with anxiety over
Jenny's distress, wanting to get the call over, ready to
brain Belinda if the caller turned out to be a double-
glazing salesman or something of that sort.

'Mrs Kincaid?' said a deep and familiar voice in her
ear.

Amy almost dropped the instrument. Only Dr
Bentley, with whom she had worked that afternoon,
possessed such a seductive voice. What on earth was he
ringing her about, and how did he know her number,
and why, for heaven's sake, was he calling her Mrs
Kincaid? Somehow she recovered her calm.

'This is Amy Kincaid,' she said coolly in a soft, well
modulated voice. 'Can I help you?' Not letting him
know that she was aware of his identity, she felt, gave
her a small advantage.

'Amy?' said the voice in a surprised fashion. 'Nurse
Kincaid?'

'Yes.'

'I'm so sorry, I must apologise—I automatically
assumed. . . Look, Miss Kincaid, I thought, when I

decided to phone, that you might be related to Jenny,
since your name isn't too common, but I had no idea
that. . .' there was a pause. . .'I thought I was going to
speak to a Mrs Kincaid, Jenny's mother. The last thing
I want to do is embarrass you.'

Later, Amy realised just how dense she had been,
assuming that Max Bentley knew that Jenny was her
sister, and that their mother was dead. He had thought
she was a single parent and that Jenny was her
daughter.

Ignorant as to how his mind was working, she said in
her quiet, slightly husky voice, 'I'm not embarrassed,
Dr Bentley, just surprised that you should know Jenny
and want to speak to me about her.'

'You obviously don't know that Jenny's at school with
my two children, Rose and Harry—that's why I'm
ringing.'

'Oh, a rose by any other name! I had no idea that the
pretty Rose Jenny has spoken of is your daughter. They
seem to have got to know each other well in the few
days they've been at Campion's,' Amy told him.

'Exactly. That's one of the things I wanted to mention. You must know that Rose is partially deaf and is
rather timid. I have to thank Jenny for having
befriended her and helped make school life easier for
her—it's really been wonderful, and a great relief to me.
Of course, having met you and worked with you today,
I can see where Jenny gets her practical sympathy and
charm from.'

'Well, thank you, Dr Bentley.' Amy felt herself blushing and was glad the sophisticated doctor couldn't see
her. He would probably find it amusing that a young
woman could so easily be affected by a few complimen-
tary words. 'It's kind of you to phone and say all these

nice things about Jenny. I'll tell her you're pleased about her friendship with Rose.'

'That's not all I was phoning about,' Max told her. 'I wonder if you can let me have the recipe for the cakes they had for afternoon break. My children are raving about them, and I've no idea what they are. I thought I'd try my hand at making a batch.'

For the first time since the conversation began, Amy felt at ease. She burst out laughing. The picture she conjured up of the elegant doctor bustling around the kitchen making peanut butter and banana cookies she found hilarious.

'What's so funny?' he asked plaintively. 'I'm not bad in the kitchen, you know.'

'I'm sure you're not,' replied Amy, suppressing further laughter. 'But they're awfully messy to prepare.'

'But what are they, dear girl? Please tell!'

Amy rather liked the way he said 'dear girl', it sounded as if they were old friends. 'Peanut butter and banana,' she told him, smiling into the phone.

'Oh, yuk—sounds revolting!'

'Still want to try to make some?'

'Certainly, I'll enjoy the challenge. Will you kindly send the recipe via the children?'

'Of course. Goodnight, Dr Bentley.'

'Goodnight, Miss Kincaid, and thank you.'

Amy stood for a few moments in the hall getting over the surprise of his call and the knowledge that he must live nearby. Her firm resolve to be just on good working terms with her colleagues was going to take some living up to. Away from the Health Centre it was definitely going to be more difficult to think of him just as a doctor.

Inevitably she would meet up with him now that his

children and Jenny had become friends. Would she be able to maintain a calm detachment with someone as handsome and masculine as Dr Bentley? She prayed that she would. She was only too well aware of her ineptness where men were concerned. Even hearing his voice had made her blush.

If she was honest with herself, all afternoon in his clinic she had been conscious of his presence, his strong virile presence. Working, and being absorbed in her work and his medical expertise, had made it relatively easy to ignore her awareness of him. But whether she would be able to pretend to be indifferent if their paths crossed frequently outside of work, she didn't know.

Of course, her best protection would be his probable indifference to her as a woman. She sighed to herself. It was a foregone conclusion that he would see her only as Jenny's elder sister, fairly domesticated, good for pinching recipes from, and a reliable nurse. She had nothing to worry about; he would make sure that their relationship remained on a cool and friendly basis.

Well, she would be happy with that, she assured herself as she opened the kitchen door. In fact it was exactly what she wanted—a nice straightforward friendship with a man, and no strings attached. Something she had found impossible to achieve in the past with men.

Unnoticed, Amy stood in the doorway and breathed a sigh of relief. Jenny was quite restored to her usual happy self; she was grating cheese. Belinda, for the moment exuding charm and warmth, was sculpting tomatoes into pretty shapes to decorate their beans on toast. They were both laughing at some remark that Belinda had made.

Suddenly Amy was overwhelmed by the blissfully

harmonious beauty of the scene—her two pretty sisters preparing supper in the delightful kitchen of the aptly named 'Doll's House', a small terraced cottage on the village green. The kitchen-cum-dining-room was, in fact, quite sizeable. The previous owner had added an extension, and a large bay window with lead light windows pushed out into the courtyard garden. The low-beamed ceiling emphasised the length of the room, and the amber-shaded wall lights reflected back from the white surfaces between the beams and support timbers.

Belinda looked up and saw Amy. 'Well,' she asked, 'who's old sexy voice, then?'

'Dr Bentley. He's the father of two new children who started school with Jenny.'

'Oh, great! Isn't he nice?' said Jenny.

'I didn't know you'd met him,' said Amy, surprised.

'He came to get Rose and Harry from school today while I was waiting for you,' Jenny explained.

'Oh,' said Belinda, losing some of her animation. 'He's a dad, then. Why didn't their mother fetch them from school?'

'They haven't got a mummy. She went away, and she died, I think—Rose isn't sure, she was only a baby when it happened.'

'Oh, really?' said Belinda, brightening up.

'How sad!' murmured Amy, wondering which of the many tales that were circulating the Health Centre about the doctor were true. She resolved not to tell her sisters at present that she was working with Dr Bentley. It seemed especially important that Belinda shouldn't be privy to this fact.

'How old is he, then, this Dr Bentley?' asked Belinda as they sat down to supper.

Jenny looked thoughtful. 'Oh, quite old, I should think,' she said after a moment. 'He's got grey hair, but he's very nice. I like him, and Rose and Harry love him very much.'

'Good,' said Amy firmly. 'That's all that matters.'

Belinda gave her a hard look from her beautiful violet eyes. 'He might not be that old,' she said. 'He didn't sound old.'

'Well, one way or the other I don't suppose it will affect us at all.' Amy started to collect up the dirty plates.

'You never know,' said Belinda, her mouth quirking into a smile. 'I quite go for older men!'

After Jenny had gone to bed, and Belinda had retired to shampoo her hair, put on a face pack, and massage herself with aromatic oils, Amy sat down to write out the recipe for Dr Bentley.

It was lovely in the kitchen. The solid fuel Aga that was a bore to stoke up, but a blessing to cook and warm the house by, made faint sounds as the coke shifted and settled. The solid old refectory table and ladderback chairs, that had been in the family for years, almost filled the window recess, and looked gracious and homely at the same time. It was at this table that Amy sat writing out her recipe.

She included a short note in her neat rounded hand, because it was unlikely that she would see the doctor tomorrow.

Dear Dr Bentley,

Enclosed as requested the recipe for peanut butter and banana cakes. They may sound revolting, but, made with wholemeal flour and sweetened with honey, they're both nutritious and tasty. So pleased to know that your children enjoyed them.

Do let me know if you have any problems.

Yours sincerely,

Amy Kincaid.

There was much else that she would like to have written, but it all seemed superfluous. She put letter and recipe in an envelope, sealed it up and tucked it into the flap of Jenny's school bag.

Suddenly very tired, she put out the lights and took herself off to bed in her tiny room, after looking in on Jenny and making sure she was asleep.

CHAPTER THREE

AMY dropped Jenny off at school a little early the following morning, then went back to the cottage to pick up Belinda, who had to be at college for a lecture at nine-thirty.

'You should have been ready to come with me when I took Jenny to school,' said Amy crossly, after she had waited for five minutes for Belinda to appear.

'But I don't have to get there till nine-thirty, there's bags of time,' shrugged Belinda. She looked bright and pretty, if a little odd, in a long black skirt, boots, a multi-coloured jumper and a shapeless black felt hat jammed down over her fair curls.

'It's going to take me ten minutes to go round the town and drop you off,' grumbled Amy. 'And I've got a job to go to, remember.'

'As if you'd ever let me forget!' sulked Belinda.

In spite of the diversion, Amy got to the centre in good time and parked at the rear of the building in the staff car park. She was just about to buzz for admission at the side door when it was opened by Dr Bentley. He looked tired and haggard, but produced a nice smile.

'Do come in, Nurse,' he said, pulling the door wide open and pressing himself against the wall to give her room. 'I'm just off—early rounds. Did you, by the way, send me the recipe?'

'Yes, of course. I said I would.'

'You did indeed—thank you.' His rather stern mouth quirked at the corners.

Amy wondered if he was laughing at her; she wished

she could say something bright and clever, as Belinda would, but she couldn't think of anything, except to remark that he looked tired. She said it without thinking, and blushed afterwards.

'Well, I am a bit,' he said cheerfully. 'I was on call last night and there seemed to be any number of emergencies.'

Before she could stop herself, Amy asked, 'What do you do about the children when you're on call?'

'Mrs Carter from the lodge comes up and sleeps in, She's very good, and it's only a temporary measure till things get back to normal.'

'Oh, good.' He was still standing in the doorway, and Amy had to squeeze past him to get through. 'I must get on,' she explained.

'Yes, of course,' he agreed smiling down at her. 'See you later.' He let himself out into the car park.

Amy was on bloods and ECGs that day, and there were a lot of them to do. The waiting area outside the clinic-room was full all the morning, with patients booked in and those sent from various doctors after examination. She only just finished by twelve-thirty, the latest collection time for the bloods to be sent to the local hospital laboratory.

There were three ECGs to do that afternoon before she went off duty at three o'clock. She collected a sandwich from the delicatessen in the High Street and found a seat in the Cathedral Close where she could sit and eat it in peace. She closed her eyes after she had eaten. Ten minutes, she thought, basking in the mild autumn sunlight that filtered through the red leaves still hanging on the trees, delighting in the warmth that caressed her skin.

She almost dozed off. It was so quiet and tranquil in

the shadow of the magnificent Cathedral spire, surrounded by the lichen-covered grey cloisters.

The peace was suddenly broken by the loud and angry barking of dogs. Amy opened her eyes. Two quite small dogs, one a Yorkshire terrier, the other a Jack Russell, were snarling and yapping at each other ferociously. Each was trying to bite the other. Their owners, an elderly lady and a small boy, stood helplessly by, watching and shrieking at them.

Suddenly the boy darted forward and tried to grab the Jack Russell. Both dogs seemed to turn on him at once, and he screeched with pain as one of them bit him.

A crowd began to gather, but nobody did anything. The boy, in spite of being hurt, was trying to separate the animals. Amy left her seat and ran towards the fighting dogs. She tore off her anorak as she ran, and threw it over the two dogs as she reached the scene. She pulled the boy away. 'Let me look,' she said, holding up his bloodstained hand. The boy stared at her. 'I'm a nurse,' she explained. 'I can help.'

'But what about Sam?' wailed the boy. 'He'll get hurt!'

Both dogs were concealed beneath Amy's jacket. They were still snarling, but in a subdued fashion; the sudden descent of the anorak must have given them a fright. The elderly lady, at that point, pulled her tiny Yorkshire terrier out of the fracas. She looked pale and frightened and on the verge of collapse.

Amy told the boy to put a lead on his dog. 'Look,' she said, 'the surgery where I work is only just across the square. Let's go over and take a look at you both.'

Somebody gave the lady a supporting arm and followed Amy, leading the dog, who seemed to be none the worse for the fight.

'Oh,' exclaimed the elderly lady, 'so this is the new surgery! My doctor's here now.'

Amy breathed a sigh of relief. It helped that at least one of the patients was on the list of a resident doctor. There were so many rules and regulations these days, tied up with indemnity insurances, that one had to be careful about who was treated on the premises.

Her relief was even greater when the boy—who told her his name was Martin—said nervously, 'Cripes, my Uncle James works here! He won't half be mad about this!' He waved his bitten hand about, causing it to ooze more blood. 'He doesn't like dogs, especially Sam.'

Amy grabbed at his hand, holding it aloft again and applying pressure to the uneven wound, as she conducted her little party into reception.

There was only one receptionist and one pharmacist on duty from twelve-thirty to two, when most of the doctors and many other staff were at lunch. Gina Smart was on the phone when Amy and the others entered. She stared at them for a moment, then spoke hastily into the mouthpiece. 'Look, I'll ring you back, Mr Long, we've got an emergency here.'

Amy said apologetically, 'Not exactly an emergency, Gina, but these two people need help.' She expained about the dog fight.

'You say Mrs Lennox is a patient of Dr Hool?' queried Gina.

'Yes.'

Gina flicked on the VDU and brought up a list of patients beginning with L on the screen. 'Mrs Vera Lennox, 19 Shipton Street?'

Amy repeated this to Mrs Lennox, who nodded.

'Right,' said Gina. 'Well, Dr Hool isn't in, but Dr Bentley, who's a partner in that practice, is. I'll give him a buzz, I'm sure he'll see you, Mrs Lennox.'

She gave the patient a nice smile while she waited for the doctor to answer the phone.

Amy thought, poor man, he's been out on call all night, perhaps he's trying to snatch a breather.

The phone crackled into life as it was answered from one of the consultation-rooms. Gina explained the situation, and Amy heard Max Bentley's voice clearly agreeing to see Mrs Lennox. To her surprise, she then heard Gina telling him about the boy Martin.

'There,' said the receptionist, looking pleased with herself, 'our Dr Bentley is going to see Martin too!' She shrugged. 'Well, there isn't another doctor on the premises at this time, and I don't want you dripping blood all over the carpet,' she finished in a friendly fashion, smiling at the boy.

'Martin's related to someone who works here,' Amy told her. 'James someone. Any idea who that might be?'

'What's your surname?' Gina asked Martin.

'Marshall.'

'Oh no!', groaned Gina. 'Not related to Dr Marshall, are you?'

'He's my uncle.'

Gina raised her eyes heavenward. 'He doesn't like dogs,' she said, looking at a now quiet Sam and even quieter Rolf, the Yorkshire terrier.

'I know,' agreed Martin gloomily. 'I don't have to wait and see him, do I?'

'Not if you don't want to.'

Martin shook his head emphatically. 'I don't.'

'Well, it'll be up to you to square Dr Bentley,' said Gina. 'He may feel you ought to see your uncle when he comes in, but he'll see to you now.'

'Great! I bet he'll be OK.'

Amy escorted Mrs Lennox and Martin up in the lift to the first floor, and along the carpeted corridor to B suite, where Drs Makepeace, Hool and Bentley had their rooms.

To her tap on the door, his deep voice invited her to come in. 'If you would please look at the boy first, Doctor,' she requested. 'I think he just needs a pressure dressing which I can do, and an anti-tetanus if he's not up to date with his injections, though I dare say he is, since he's at school.'

Max Bentley, who still looked tired but was now shaven and less haggard than when she had seen him that morning, gave her a lopsided smile. 'I'm superflu-ous, Nurse, really aren't I? You've obviously correctly diagnosed and decided treatment. Are you simply asking for a second opinion?'

Amy felt her cheeks grow red with embarrassment. She hadn't meant to sound so cocksure of herself. It seemed that always her instinct, allied with training at one of the best hospitals, made it impossible for her not to assess and act quickly.

'I'm sorry, Doctor, I shouldn't diagnose. My apolo-gies, but will you please see Martin first?'

Max felt sorry for her. How could such an attractive woman, well trained and with a child of her own, be so vulnerable to the slighest comment? 'I'm sure you're right, Nurse,' he said in a kindly fashion. 'I wasn't criticising your judgement. Let's have the boy in at once.'

Martin came in, holding his damaged hand up with his good one, and looking as if butter wouldn't melt in his mouth.

'If you please, sir,' he said, looking Max Bentley straight in the eye, 'I'd be awfully grateful if you don't say anything to my uncle about this. He's very anti-dog, and especially anti-Sam. He might even want to have him put down.'

'Your uncle is Dr Marshall, I presume,' said Max, his lips twitching as he tried not to smile at the boy's earnestness. 'Where's the canine terror now, then.'

'Oh, he's with Mrs Lennox,' said Martin. 'He and Rolf—that's her dog—are all right together now.'

'Hrmph,' said Dr Bentley. 'Right, let's have a look at this hand.' He examined the jagged wound, made worse because Martin had tried to snatch his hand away from the dog's jaws and torn his flesh in the process. 'Well, I agree with Nurse Kincaid, and you're jolly lucky she was on the spot—the wound just needs antiseptic and a dressing. It should heal within a week or so. Your anti-tetanus injections are up to date, I presume?'

'Yes, sir,' said Martin smartly. He squinted sideways at the doctor. 'My uncle,' he queried, 'will he have to know?'

'You tell him,' replied Max. 'In your own time.'

'Gosh, that's brilliant!'

'Possibly,' said Max drily. 'Now off you go with Nurse, she'll see to your hand.' He turned to Amy. 'Be good enough to show Mrs Lennox in, will you, before taking Master Marshall away and dressing that hand.' He smiled at her, a smile that reached his cool grey eyes, and warmed them in some inexplicable way. 'Come back when you've finished.'

'Yes, Doctor,' she said, deliberately prim.

Mrs Lennox had already improved now that the shock was over, but she was extremely breathless, and complained of 'palpitations'—not surprising, since she had a history of mild angina and occasional asthma attacks.

Dr Bentley examined her thoroughly, and gave her a prescription for a new, improved inhaler, to ward off her asthma. When Amy returned, he asked her to take Mrs Lennox along to the clinic-room and mix her a small glucose drink. 'One of my special cocktails,' he explained with a smile. 'I see you don't live too far away—I think you'll feel fit enough to finish Rolf's walk in a short while. But do stay in reception until you feel ready to leave.'

'Isn't he nice?' said Mrs Lennox a few minutes later, sitting in the clinic-room drinking her 'cocktail'. 'I shall ask to see him again when I come.'

'He's an excellent doctor,' agreed Amy, knowing her reply must sound stiff and inadequate, and wishing she could sound more enthusiastic. It was all part of the wall of reserve that she had built around herself since first Gordon and then Bill had let her down so badly. She didn't want anything to shatter her hardly won peace. And this desire made her shy away from admitting, even privately, that Max Bentley interested her.

'I meant he's a nice man too,' persisted Mrs Lennox. 'Not brisk and stuck up like some doctors I could mention,' she added in a dry tone.

This time Amy agreed in a much warmer fashion. Later in the afternoon, when she was preparing the equipment for her last ECG patient, she recalled that Max had been described to her as possessing those very qualities when she first arrived at the centre. Well, that certainly wasn't true, as she'd soon discovered, in fact all the little things that she was finding out about him made him increasingly human and likeable.

It was after four o'clock when she finally left the centre. The car park at the back of St Anne's House, where the staff had their own parking area, was full—more than full. Somebody had parked outside the lines in the public park, obstructing Amy's egress from the private park.

'Oh no, I don't believe it,' she muttered, staring at the gap between vehicles even too small for her to

manoeuvre her tiny Fiat. She looked round for a
moment, hoping the driver was about to return. No
such luck—nobody appeared to claim the car. Amy
rang the bell at the side door of the centre. She would
have to phone the school and ask the Campions to tell
Jenny she would be late picking her up. How late? she
wondered. How long would it be before the owner of the
car returned?

Gina let her in and Amy explained what had happened. 'What?' wailed Gina. 'What a damned nuisance!
The doctors won't be able to get out in an emergency.'

Amy, her thoughts full of Jenny being disappointed
about being collected late from school, hadn't thought
of that.

'Do you think we'd better let the police know, or the
traffic warden? They should be able to do something
about it.'

'Yes, clamp it, probably, then where would we be?'

'You could ask if it's any of the patients' who are
waiting,' suggested Amy. 'One of them might be
responsible.'

'Good thinking. What make and colour is the car?'

'It's a pretty ancient Mini, blue, well looked after.
That's all I can say. I could go and check the registra-
tion number, but it will be obvious if it belongs to
anybody here.'

Gina switched on her microphone. 'Will the owner of
the blue Mini parked in the public car park at the rear
of the building please contact the reception desk. You're
obstructing the exit of cars from the staff park.'

She and Amy waited. No one in the waiting-rooms
stirred, no one came down in the lift or by the stairs
from the upper floors.

The internal phone rang. It was Max Bentley. 'I was

in the waiting area up here and heard your message over the intercom,' he said. 'Any response?'

'No, Dr Bentley.'

'Right, I'll be down shortly with someone—a dinky car like that is easily moved. Hang on before you do anything more official, will you?'

'Yes, of course.' The receptionist turned to Amy. 'Did you hear that?'

'Yes, I wonder what he means to do about it?'

A few minutes later Max Bentley, with Tom Conrad and Craig Thompson, both large, beefy doctors from another practice, stepped out of the lift.

'Right, Gina, lead us to the offending vehicle,' said Tom Conrad. All three men were looking pleased with themselves, presumably at the thought of a bit of physical effort, even the cool sophisticated Dr Bentley.

'Amy will show you,' said Gina. 'It was she who found her way blocked when she wanted to leave.'

'In a hurry?' asked Max as they all filed out through the side door.

'Yes, I am rather,' Amy agreed.

'Have you to pick up Jenny from school?'

'Yes, though the Campions are very good and are happy for her to remain there till I arrive. But I hate to think of her having to wait.'

'I'm sure you do. It must be difficult coping with a small girl and a job, even with your sister's help.'

The way he had phrased his remark confirmed Amy's suspicion that he thought Jenny was her daughter. She was about to open her mouth to explain, when they reached the end of the staff park and the offending Mini.

'Women drivers!' said Craig in disgust.

'How do you know it's a woman driver?' asked Amy crossly. 'It could just as easily be a man, you've no right to assume it's a woman.'

Both he and Tom Conrad laughed out loud, and even Max's mouth quirked at the corners as if he were suppressing a laugh.

Amy turned on him. 'And I thought better of you!' she snapped accusingly, prompted by some unknown need to vent her anger on him in particular. 'I didn't think you'd sink low enough to join the ranks of the other male chauvinists round here.'

He looked a bit taken aback, then frowned in a puzzled fashion. The other two doctors just continued laughing, though in a rather less boisterous fashion.

'My goodness, we *are* cross, aren't we?' said Tom and Craig in chorus, as if they'd rehearsed the line.

'Oh, don't be so bloody patronising!' Amy was thoroughly exasperated with their childish behaviour. It seemed incredible to think they were responsible doctors. The annoying thing was, they were good doctors. Why, she thought irritably, do men, even those who should know better, descend to this level in their determination to undermine women?

'Look, I suggest we get on with this,' said Max mildly. He clearly wasn't going to be drawn for or against either Amy or his colleagues.

All three doctors took off their jackets and handed them to Amy, the two younger men still apparently finding the situation amusing.

Together, using the bumpers which on a Mini were designed to take the strain, they heaved and manoeuvred the small vehicle away from the gateway to the Health Centre car park.

Both Dr Thompson and Dr Conrad were young, muscular, rugby-playing men, who looked capable of moving anything by brute force, but Amy was surprised by Dr Bentley's toughness. He looked lean and fit, but hardly a match for the other two, yet divested of his jacket, he revealed broad, powerful shoulders and biceps that bulged hugely under his white shirt-sleeves. She noted with interest, too, that he was sweating less profusely than the others.

'Hey, what d'ya think you're doin' with my car?' came a bellow from the end of the car park, and a burly-looking man who wouldn't have disgraced the strong man slot in a circus charged towards them.

The three doctors all looked astonished, and, Amy was sure, embarrassed. She got into her clapped-out Fiat, checked that it was in neutral, and switched on the engine, which accommodatingly started at once. 'Good girl!' she breathed, as she changed into first gear and started to move smoothly out of the parking area. She wound down the window, just as the irate owner of the Mini arrived. She smiled sweetly at Max, Tom and Graig. 'Women drivers,' she said, and moved quietly away.

Amy collected Jenny from school. She hadn't minded waiting and had got involved in the preparations for the Nativity Play to be held at the end of term.

'The boarders,' Jenny explained to her big sister, 'do most of the main parts, and I s'pose that's only right, because they're here all the time. Day pupils do the other parts.'

'Well, that sounds fair enough,' said Amy, who knew the drill, having been educated as a boarder in a convent school.

'I'd like to have been the Virgin Mary,' said Jenny wistfully, 'but I'm an angel instead.'

'I think being an angel is pretty good.'

'Yes, and we don't have to say anything—well, except Michael, the chief angel, so I suggested that Rose should be an angel too,' explained Jenny.

'And is she going to be?'

'Oh, yes, Mrs Campion thought it was a good idea, as long as she stands next to me, and I hold her hand.'

Amy wasn't sure how she felt about this. It seemed that Jenny was almost the only contact that Rose had at school. She didn't know how good this was for Rose, but wondered if it was fair to Jenny.

'Who's going to be the Angel Gabriel?' she asked.

'Harry.'

Yes, well, he would be, thought Amy, if he has anything like his father's poise and self-sufficiency.

'Not one of the boarders, then?' she asked.

'Silly, there aren't any boy boarders,' said Jenny.

To make up for being late collecting her, Amy took Jenny across the Green to the village shop. This had half moved with the times in so far as it had self-service stands and shelves, but maintained its older function of supplying paraffin and Calor gas, hen feed and vegetables, logs and firewood. There was also a flourishing sub-post office and an off-licence on the large premises.

Jenny loved the village shop, and so did Amy. It seemed strong and ongoing, as if nothing would divert it no matter what modern inventions hit the village. Like the pub opposite, the Old House, it was timeless.

Amy loved the smell of the shop, a mixture of chicken feed, paraffin, and rubber from the wellingtons suspended by string from a beam. Jenny loved the racks of children's books with their bright covers, the tiny plastic dolls and animals in boxes sitting on the shelves with jigsaw puzzles and paintboxes, and the endless variety of new sweets, as well as some of the old ones that the shop boasted.

'I'd like some caramel custards,' said Jenny, 'and

may I have one of the new jigsaw puzzles, a Christmassy one?'

'It's only October!' protested Amy. 'We haven't even had Hallowe'en or Guy Fawkes Night!'

'Well, can I have some fireworks ready for November the fifth?'

'What about a mask for Hallowe'en?' suggested Amy.

While Jenny was deliberating between the merits of a witch's face and hat, and a skeletal mask, the old-fashioned doorbell clanged, and Max Bentley, followed by two dark-haired, pretty children, entered.

Max strode down the shop till he reached Amy. 'I'm so glad I've caught up with you,' he said in a fierce whisper. 'Don't you think it's time we discussed your child's needs and did something about them?'

Amy stared at him open-mouthed. He sounded almost belligerent, as if she'd done something wrong.

She retorted equally fiercely in a low voice, 'I don't know what you're talking about, Dr Bentley, and *if* I did, I should probably tell you it had nothing to do with you.' She looked to see if Jenny or the other children had noticed anything amiss, but they were excitedly examining the Hallowe'en goodies and oblivious of the adults.

'I thought you had an arrangement with the Campions for Jenny to stay at school until you collected her, but I understand from your sister that this isn't always so.'

'My sister?' queried Amy.

'Belinda.' He gave her an exasperated look. 'I gave her a lift. She'd expected you'd pick her up at college, but when you didn't she called at the Health Centre, thinking you were still there. When she'd found you'd left early, she thought you'd gone shopping and that Jenny would be alone in the house. She was most

anxious to get home to see that all was well. She
certainly didn't know of any arrangement for tonight for
Jenny to stay at school.'

Amy gritted her teeth. Belinda up to her old tricks
again, she guessed, making her look irresponsible or
uncaring—but why? She looked up into Max Bentley's
steely grey eyes and knew she didn't have to look further
for a reason. A handsome, distinguished man. How
Belinda had found out so quickly that he was a doctor
at the centre, she didn't know, but having done so, she
certainly hadn't lost any time in furthering an
acquaintance.

When the doctor had phoned about the recipe, Amy
hadn't mentioned that she knew him, letting her sisters
believe the connection was only through the school.
Instinct, perhaps, making her wary of Belinda's reaction
to the fact.

Well, she'd been right to be cautious, although it
hadn't done her much good. Her sister had found out
soon enough, and had already gone into action.

For there was no doubt that Belinda's turning up at
the centre was deliberate. She knew what time Amy
expected to leave, and what the arrangements were for
collecting Jenny. She was mischief-making for her own
purposes.

Obviously she wanted to get to know the doctor and
didn't want any competition from Amy. To pretend
concern for her small sister, and imply that Amy was
less concerned, would bring her to his attention in a
favourable light.

Amy's old instinct for protecting her sister made her
seek for a suitable answer to the doctor's accusation of
her own irresponsibility, without making Belinda out a
liar. Her own anger with the man died. It wasn't his
fault if he was as gullible and fell as easily under

Belinda's spell as other men. She swallowed temper and
pride.

'Well, it was kind of you to give my sister a lift home,
Doctor. As to the rest, I think it's just a question of
getting wires crossed. Belinda knows Jenny will never
be alone in the house. We always make sure one of us is
with her. Belinda just panicked, I expect.'

It was a fairly lame explanation, but on the spur of
the moment she couldn't think of anything else that
would seem to extricate both of them from the doctor's
wrath. And though in some instances she would have
been prepared to ignore a near-stranger's condem-
nation, she felt strongly about this man thinking ill of
her. It wasn't only on a personal level that she wanted
his approbation, but it was important that he approved
of her professionally.

How could he do that, she reasoned, if he thought her
an undutiful *mother*—for that he still believed her to be
Jenny's mother rather than her sister seemed implicit
in the way he had spoken. She guessed that Belinda
hadn't tried to make this plain, for her own peculiar
reasons.

Amy took a deep breath. She must explain, and it
might as well be now. As she was about to open her
mouth, the three children came laughing and chattering
across to the corner where she and Max were standing.

Jenny, with her usual aplomb, said at once in her
polite, old-fashioned manner, 'Hallo, Dr Bentley, I'm
glad you've met my sister Amy; now I don't have to
introduce you.'

Max breathed in rather hard, and said in his most
velvet voice, 'Your sister,' there was some emphasis on
the 'sister', 'and I work together at the Health Centre,
Jenny, that's how we know each other, but Amy hasn't
met my son and daughter.' He gave Jenny a lovely

smile, to which she responded in an engaging manner. 'Perhaps you'd like to perform that introduction.'

'Yes, please. Amy, this is Rose. When you speak to her you must let her see your face, because she's rather deaf.' Amy nodded, made speechless by her young sister's understanding. 'And this,' continued Jenny, 'is Harry.'

Amy crouched down on her heels so that she was on a level with Rose. 'How do you do,' she said plainly. 'Jenny's told me so much about you.'

Rose hung her head and then looked up at Amy through long dark lashes. 'She's told me a lot about you too,' she whispered.

Harry stepped forward and held out his hand. 'Hello,' he said. 'I'm Harry.' He looked at her with clear grey eyes just like his father's.

Amy straightened up and gave him her hand. 'I'm Amy,' she said. 'How do you do.' She thought, he's stoical—has to be, because he feels responsible for his sister. I wonder if he feels pushed out on her account?

Over the heads of the children, she and Max faced each other, eye to eye.

Max's mouth quirked at the corners, his grey eyes remarkably soft and tender. 'I'm so sorry—I must apologise. I've made so many rash judgements. I might have known, even on our brief acquaintance, that you wouldn't neglect your duties in any way. The children, as always, seem to have understood better than I.'

'Out of the mouths of babes. . .' Amy quoted.

'How true,' he said, sounding rather sad. 'Perhaps we should listen more, or at any rate I should.'

Amy shrugged. 'We all should,' she said softly. 'Not always, but sometimes children go to the heart of the matter.' She moved to the counter to pay for Jenny's purchases. 'Goodnight, Dr Bentley,' she said, as they left, and the old-fashioned bell clanged behind them.

She and Jenny walked hand in hand across the Green, Jenny skipping up and down with excitement. 'I do like living here,' she said, smiling up at Amy. 'I like my school and our little doll's house cottage, and the Bentleys. Even Dr Bentley, though he looks rather stern sometimes. Do you like all those things too?'

'Oh, yes, I do,' said Amy, smiling in the darkness, and looking up at the canopy of stars that filled the autumn night sky. 'I like all those things very much.' Especially, she said to herself, the rather stern Dr Bentley.

CHAPTER FOUR

AMY had intended to challenge Belinda for misleading Dr Bentley about their arrangements for Jenny, but she was reluctant to spoil the happy mood that she and her little sister had enjoyed walking back from the shop. She decided to ignore the incident, and hope that such a situation was not repeated.

Belinda was sitting on the stairs talking on the telephone when Amy and Jenny let themselves into the tiny hall.

'Hi,' she mouthed at them, with a dimpling smile, 'won't be long, I've started getting supper—jacket potatoes, cheese and salad, OK?'

Amy knew from long experience that Belinda was trying to charm her into overlooking her behaviour at the Health Centre, should she have learned of the matter, by being caring and helpful. The best thing was to behave as if she knew nothing, or was biding her time about tackling the matter.

It gave her some satisfaction to see, during the course of the evening, that Belinda was a little uncomfortable, wondering whether Amy was in the know about her actions. She relaxed, however, as the evening wore on, and the three of them played a noisy game of Junior Trivial Pursuit before Jenny went off to bed.

Amy ignored her sister's attempts to find out if she knew anything. She used Belinda's own trick of smiling innocence to deflect the oblique questions directed at her, until Belinda gave up and they both retired for the night.

'Well, at least,' Amy said to herself, just before drifting off to sleep, 'Max Bentley isn't likely to be fooled for long by Belinda's blandishments. He's too sophisticated and mature for that.'

Her last thoughts, as she feel asleep, were of the doctor, talking to her in the village shop, looking slightly baffled, and at the same time pleased, as little Jenny said, 'This is my sister Amy.' His luminous grey eyes had gleamed with humour as he'd apologised for mistaking the situation.

Still keeping up the charm, Belinda was up and ready to accompany Amy and Jenny to school and then on to Castleminster the next morning. Clearly she wasn't going to risk making Amy angry by being late a second time. She was, for her, subdued, though cheerful. Unasked, she got out of the car to accompany Jenny up the drive to the main house when they arrived.

Jenny turned to give Amy a kiss. She raised her tiny smudges of eyebrows and whispered, 'Why is Belinda being so nice? Is there a MAN about somewhere?'

'Don't be cheeky,' said Amy repressively, hiding a smile and her surprise at the pertinence of Jenny's remark. It was true that Belinda put on an angelic act when a personable man was around, though on this occasion she was probably paving the way for an apology should it emerge that she had given misleading information to Dr Bentley. It was an old trick of hers, to turn on the charm and build up goodwill when she felt herself to be in danger of being found out in deception.

Max Bentley chose that moment to drive up with Harry and Rose. He smiled at all three of the Kincaid sisters, bestowing, Amy thought, his charm equally between them. He said goodbye to his children, then turned to Amy and Belinda.

'I have to do a couple of visits just out of town,' he said kindly, looking at Amy, 'before going to St Anne's. Would it help if I dropped Belinda off at college, which is on my route, to save you going out of your way?'

'Thank you, that would be lovely,' replied Amy, metaphorically gritting her teeth as Belinda, all smiles, dragged her bag out of the Fiat and slid, showing a great deal of shapely leg, into the doctor's raunchy-looking Range Rover.

Max Bentley gave Amy a polite smile. 'My pleasure— glad to have been of service,' he murmured.

Amy nodded. There was really nothing else she could say. He had looked with obvious admiration at Belinda's legs as she climbed into his car.

Well, thought Amy as she drove smartly away from the school gates, what healthy male wouldn't? She didn't often envy her sister, but just for a moment she wished she too had legs up to her waist, and was being driven to work by Max Bentley.

Amy was grateful that St Anne's was so busy that morning, that she had no time to think. She was on duty in the baby clinic, weighing in and recording infants recently delivered, giving vaccines and advising young mums about feeding routines.

At the end of the morning she felt drained—so many babies, so many mothers and occasional fathers, needing help and advice. The room felt hot and stuffy and she had a slight but nagging headache.

The last baby was brought in accompanied by both parents. They were young, obviously very much in love, and over the moon about their three-week-old son. They were proud and happy, and everything that a young couple should be with their first baby, and yet some sixth sense told Amy that all was not well.

'Jim took time off from work,' explained Mrs Cole, 'to come with me, as it's my first visit to the clinic.' She looked pleased, but, Amy thought, rather pale, tired and edgy. Even her hair looked lank and lifeless.

'How lovely,' smiled Amy. 'It's nice to see a dad taking a real interest in his baby.'

'I'm going to do everything for him the same as if it was Tracy doing it,' explained the young man.

'Good,' said Amy. 'Your wife looks as if she could do with a rest. Perhaps you could take baby Jonathan out this afternoon so that Mrs Cole can have a nap.' She turned to the young woman. 'How are you sleeping?' she asked.

Her husband answered before she could do so. 'Well, she doesn't sleep very well, and that's a fact. Worries about the baby in case something should happen to him—and then,' he hesitated and looked anxiously at his wife, 'she's got this cough, you see. Even if I get up to see to Jonathan, she wakes up and coughs like mad.'

'Jim,' said his wife, sounding frightened, 'you prom-ised you wouldn't tell about my cough. Honestly, Nurse, it isn't anything much. I just get a tickle in my throat sometimes. It's nothing that will hurt the baby.' She looked and sounded anxious.

'Well, I'm sure it isn't,' said Amy in a soothing manner, wondering why the young woman was so frightened. 'But if you have got a cough, it would make sense to get some treatment for it. After all, a lot of people have got coughs and colds at this time of year. But it's only fair to the baby to do something about it.'

Mrs Cole looked near to tears. 'They won't take Jonathan away from me, will they?' she asked tremu-lously. 'I couldn't bear that. I'm ever so careful, when I feed him or do anything for him, not to breathe on him.'

'Good heavens, of course nobody's going to take

Jonathan away just because you have a cough! Now, let's make arrangements for you to see your doctor and get something done about it as soon as possible. Who's your GP?'

'It's somebody new, I haven't seen him before—he's taken over from Dr Roberts. Dr Roberts was ever so nice, I'd have told him about my cough, only he's retired, and I didn't want to see anyone else.'

'Oh, you'll be on Dr Bentley's list now,' said Amy, her heart bounding unaccountably at the thought of the man. 'He's a very nice doctor, and as it happens, he's a specialist on chests, so he'll have you right in no time at all. He might even be able to see you now. I'll phone and find out.'

'Dr Bentley,' his receptionist said severely, when Amy made her request, 'has had a very busy morning. He's just going to lunch.'

'Please ask him to see Mrs Cole,' pleaded Amy.

'No fear! I'll get my head bitten off, he's in a foul temper.'

'Put me through, and I'll ask him,' said Amy, sounding braver than she felt. 'You can tell him I simply want to speak to him about one of his patients, you needn't know I'm going to ask him to see somebody.'

The receptionist wavered. 'Please!' begged Amy.

'Oh, all right, on your head be it.' She switched through to the doctor's consulting-room.

The doctor's deep voice came over the phone with a staccato, 'Well?'

Amy swallowed nervously. He really did sound angry. She gathered her courage and explained in a firm, quiet voice about Mrs Cole and her chesty cough, and her concern for her baby.

'Then it might be a good idea if the patient comes up to see me straight away, Nurse. You'd better come too

if there's a baby to keep an eye on—my nurse has gone
to have her lunch, lucky lady,' he added with heavy
irony, and put the phone down before she could say
more.

There really wasn't any need for her to go with the
Coles, as Mr Cole was quite capable of nursing
Jonathan while his wife was being examined, but in
view of Dr Bentley's request Amy thought it diplomatic
to put in an appearance.

They met the receptionist going off duty as they
arrived. She raised her pencilled eyebrows almost to her
hairline as she passed Amy. 'Rather you than me,' she
whispered. 'Sir is very cross indeed.'

Amy made a face too, then went boldly to the
consulting-room door and knocked.

'Come,' said the doctor's voice briskly, and as she
entered, 'Where's the baby?'.

Amy explained that his father was looking after him,
and ushered Mrs Cole into the room. She hoped the
formidable Dr Bentley would be less curt with the young
mother than he was with her. She need not have
worried. He was gentle, kind and reassuring.

'You have an attack of acute bronchitis, Mrs Cole,'
he explained after examining her carefully. 'Have you
coughed up anything from your chest?'

Mrs Cole, who had begun to relax a little under Dr
Bentley's gentle hands, looked suddenly frightened
again. 'No,' she said quickly. 'No, I haven't coughed up
anything.'

Max stood back from the couch and nodded to Amy.
'Help Mrs Cole get dressed, Nurse, please,' he said
quietly. He moved to the window and looked out,
turning his broad back to the room, while Amy performed this task.

He turned round after a few minutes and smiled at

the patient. 'Now, Mrs Cole,' he said, 'you are going to tell me what's bothering you, and why you're so frightened.' He leaned forward and patted the girl's arm. 'You see, my dear, I know from what I can hear through this—' he indicated his stethoscope '—that you must be coughing up something, or swallowing the stuff, which is worse.'

Mrs Cole started to cry in a noiseless fashion. After a while, she stopped, sniffed, blew her nose and gave him a watery smile. 'I'm so afraid they'll take the baby, you see, if I've got a bad cough, in case he gets it too.'

'Who on earth's been filling your head with this rubbish?' he asked. Mrs Cole shook her head. 'Well, don't take any notice of them, whoever it is. Now I'm going to give you some medicine to help your cough, and also some benzoin and menthol to use as an inhalation. You simply put a few drops in a bowl, pour on hot water, and sit with your head over the steam for ten minutes at a time. You'll be surprised at how much relief it will give you.'

'Thank you, Doctor!' sighed Tracy Cole.

'I'm also going to arrange for you to have a chest X-ray—but don't be alarmed, this is just a precaution. Do you breast-feed your baby?'

'Yes.'

'Splendid! Babies get some immunisation from their mother through her milk, as I'm sure you know. How often does baby wake during the night to be fed?'

'Usually only once, about two o'clock,' said Mrs Cole.

'Right, do you think your husband would feed the baby, then, if you expressed some milk earlier into a feeding bottle?'

'I'm sure he would, but I don't mind feeding Jonathan then.'

'You need a couple of undisturbed nights, my dear,

and something mild to help you sleep. That way you'll get over your bronchitis quicker and feel more normal. I'd like to ask your husband to come in and talk about this. Do you mind, Mrs Cole?'

Mrs Cole shook her head, and gazed at the doctor with large, trusting eyes, quite overwhelmed by the Bentley charm. 'Whatever you say, Doctor.'

Some twenty minutes later, the Coles had gone and Amy made to follow. She too was bowled over by the charismatic doctor, and full of admiration for his professional expertise. He had succeeded in reassuring the young parents, and expertly, without arousing hostility, examined baby Jonathan. He had also secured the happy co-operation of Mr Cole in the matter of night feeds.

Max looked at his watch as Amy was about to leave. 'When are you due back on duty?' he asked.

'In just over half an hour.'

'And I. The first of my afternoon patients is due at two.'

'Look, I'm sorry about pushing you to see the Coles, it was thoughtless of me,' Amy apologised.

'It was intelligent of you. That young woman was in quite a state, physically and mentally. Who knows what a further delay might have produced?'

'It's kind of you to take it like that,' she said.

'Think nothing of it.'

He was tidying his desk as he spoke, gathering up forms and sheafs of paper with long, competent fingers.

What lovely hands he's got, thought Amy, and felt herself go hot with embarrassment. She prayed that he hadn't noticed, and walked towards the door.

'If there's nothing else, Doctor I'll be off,' she said.

He looked up and surveyed her steadily, and she felt herself blushing yet again. 'I thought since we're both late for lunch, we might have a bite together,' he said. 'The Cathedral Arms is quite good for a quick snack. What do you say—my treat?'

The thought of spending half an hour in his company was tempting—no, more than tempting, Amy suddenly realised. It would be wonderful, exciting.

'Yes, thank you, I'd like that,' she replied, hoping he wouldn't notice her uneven breathing.

'Good. In five minutes at the front door?'

'Yes.'

He was waiting for her in reception, though she had changed in record time into wine-dark cords and a chunky mohair jacket that had cost the earth—one of the few expensive buys she had made for herself. She turned up the collar on her coat as they stepped out on to the pavement, and pushed her hands into her pockets. There was a bitter wind blowing from the east. Her head still ached slightly, but the thought of the doctor's company persuaded her to ignore this. I'll be better, she decided, after getting some fresh air.

Max Bentley took her arm as they crossed the cobbled square and Amy shivered. 'Are you sure you're warm enough?' he asked. She nodded, not trusting herself to speak, astonished by the effect his touch was having on her. I'm behaving like a lovesick teenager, she thought, and fought to get control of her wanton senses.

They walked through the Cathedral cloisters to the pub, which was half buried in the thick walls separating the Cathedral Close from its secular neighbours, and entered via steep stone steps going down to the cellar-like bar.

'You'd have thought they might ascend, don't you think?' said the doctor, a wicked gleam in his eye. 'Heavenwards, rather than down to the other place.'

'There are plenty of dog collars around. I think we're

in safe hands, Doctor.' Amy smiled up at him as they stood on the steps peering down into the smoky room, where several clerics from the Cathedral college staff were seated at a table.

'Max,' he suggested. 'We're off duty and we're neighbours. I think we should be rather less formal, don't you?'

'Yes, of course,' she agreed calmly, though she felt like singing. The babble from the bar rose up with the smoke from the log fire and swirled around them as they stood side by side on the stairs, staring at each other.

Neither moved, or spoke for a moment. Then Max's grip tightened on Amy's arm. He leaned forward so that she could hear him above the muted roar of many voices. 'I hope we're going to be good friends, Amy. The children seem to be hitting it off splendidly, don't they, and Belinda seems a nice, friendly girl.'

So that's it, mused Amy. He just invited me out to talk about Belinda. What a fool I am to think he's interested in me when my stunning sister's around. And I thought he might be old enough to be immune. What a hope! She was disgusted with herself for having given way to her imagination, believing that Max too had felt something special when they stood on the stairs. He must think me an utter fool, she thought as he guided her to a table that had just become vacant.

'Spot of luck getting a table straight away,' he said, giving her a smile that moments before she would have thought was rather special and just for her.

'Yes, very lucky.' Her cool voice came out without a tremor, rather to her own surprise; for she was angry as well as disappointed with Max for being so easily taken in by Belinda, and with herself for being taken in by him.

Max frowned. He was clearly taken aback by her

sudden flat, cold tone and changed manner. 'Are you all right?' he asked. He put a hand on her shoulder and leaned across the small table to look straight into her face. 'You look flushed.'

Amy saw a way out of the hell of having to sit and listen to him talking about Belinda. 'I feel a bit faint,' she said. 'It's hot in here—I think I'd better go back to the Clinic.'

Max continued to look at her, but now in a professional, impersonal manner. Whether he was deceived or not about her condition, she wasn't sure, but within seconds he had her on her feet and was helping her back up the stairs.

'There's no need for you to come,' she said hastily. The last thing she wanted was the doctor's professional help. 'Please go back and have something to eat—you must be starving!'

He didn't even bother to answer. His long, narrow face looked grim. He took her arm as they emerged at the top of the steps and steered her back to St Anne's House. Amy couldn't decide whether he was cross because he had seen through her deception, or because he thought she was unwell.

It was as they entered the reception area that she was conscious of feeling genuinely unwell. The nagging headache had suddenly developed into a raging torrent of pain, and all her pulses were hammering fit to burst. She could hardly believe it. It was as if all the warnings that her grandmother had given her about tempting fate had come true. One moment she was pretending to feel faint to get herself out of socialising with Dr Bentley, and a few minutes later she actually fainted.

She had never done such a thing in her life. She remembered going through the elegant front door of the Clinic and wondering why the walls seemed to be circling round her, then felt herself slipping down and down, and the doctor's arms closing tightly about her. As if from a long way off, she heard his deep voice, and the lighter voice of the receptionist, then nothing.

CHAPTER FIVE

AMY vaguely remembered the journey from the Clinic. Dr Bentley had put her into a taxi, apologising as he did so that he couldn't take her home as he had a full list of patients to see.

'It doesn't matter, I'll be fine,' she'd muttered, embarrassed by the whole situation. She was furious with herself for fainting, and not quite able to rid herself of the idea that she had brought it all on herself by pretending to be ill. Common sense told her that she couldn't produce a temperature of thirty-eight point five degrees by pretending, or conjure up the incipient headache with which she had been battling all morning; but a frisson of guilt remained.

'I've telephoned Mrs Carter, my housekeeper,' said the doctor, as he made her comfortable in the back of the car. 'She'll be waiting for you at your cottage, or will arrive soon after you do, and she'll know what to do. You get to bed, take your medicine like a good girl, and don't worry. Mrs Carter will fetch Jenny home when she collects my two, and give them all their tea.'

'My car? I shall need it for work tomorrow,' protested Amy.

'My dear girl, you won't be working for at least a week! I'll arrange something about the car. Perhaps Belinda can collect it some time.'

Amy shuddered. 'Oh no, she's only just passed her test, and treats my poor little Fiat as if it were a Porsche.'

'All right,' he said soothingly. 'Don't worry, I'll sort
everything out.'

It was lovely to feel safe and reassured, but the fact
that it was Max Bentley who was providing the reassurance was annoying, to say the least.

Janet Brown had also been reassured when Amy
bewailed the fact that she'd only been at the Centre for
a few weeks, and was already being a problem.

'Don't be such an idiot, Amy—you can't help getting
a flu bug. Bugs are no respecters of the calendar, and
strike irrespective of length of service. Now, do as Max
says, go home and go to bed.' The manager had patted
her arm in a motherly fashion, and Amy felt near to
tears. 'You're too valuable as a good nurse for us to risk
complications. Just get well, dear.'

By mid-afternoon of that grey late October day, Amy
was installed in her bedroom with the sloping ceilings,
at the Doll's House. As promised by Max Bentley, Mrs
Carter was waiting for her. She took the key from Amy's
trembling fingers and let them both into the cottage.

Within minutes Mrs Carter, being the trained housekeeper that she was, had discovered where everything
was kept. She sat Amy down at the kitchen table while
she stoked up the Aga, made tea, and filled a couple of
hot water bottles, all before Amy could gather her
woolly thoughts.

'Now, Nurse dear, go and have a nice hot bath,' she
instructed. 'I've run it for you, and put your nightie
over the radiator in the bathroom. Call if you need me.'

Shaking with a mixture of cold and fever, Amy
managed to bath without help. She fumbled her way
into her nightdress and scrambled into bed. The relief
of being horizontal, warm and cosseted was overwhelm-
ing. Stupid, uncontrollable tears trickled down her hot

cheeks as Mrs Carter arrived with a jug of fresh lemon juice, and the antibiotic tablets and painkillers prescribed by Dr Bentley.

'Now, the doctor said you were to have lots of fluids, so you make a start on this and then try to get some sleep. Don't worry if you don't hear me about later on—' I'll be off to fetch the children from school and take them to the Manor for tea.'

'You are kind,' whispered Amy. 'Are you sure you don't mind?'

'Well, of course I don't, Nurse. The doctor's my boss and he's given me orders, but apart from that, it's a privilege to do something for you. Your little sister Jenny has been no end of a help to our Rose. I don't know how that poor child would have managed without her.'

Her words caused Amy the tiniest twinge of disappointment. It seemed that both the doctor and his housekeeper had ulterior motives for being kind to her— he because he was attracted to Belinda, and Mrs Carter on account of Jenny's friendship with Rose. Had she not felt so ill, she might have dwelt on these facts, but in the event, she fell into a feverish sleep almost at once.

It was dark when she woke some time later. A new moon and a few stars shone eerily through the misty darkness, framed in the lattice window by the undrawn curtains. The house was very quiet. Her head still throbbed, and she was hot, sweaty and thirsty. She switched on the bedside light, and as she did so, heard the murmur of voices and the front door being opened. There were feet on the stairs, and a moment later Belinda, eyes bright, blonde hair a tangle of damp curls, erupted into the room.

'Oh, Amy, you poor old thing! I'm so sorry you're ill. Can I do anything for you? Max says that as long as

I'm careful I won't catch your flu, or if I do, it was because I was going to get it anyway.'

Amy struggled to sit up and reach for a drink, and also focus her attention on what Belinda was saying. 'Max Bentley? Oh, I suppose you saw him when you collected Jenny, but how did you know Jenny was at the Manor?' She sipped the cool lemonade, hoping it would help clear her head.

'Max is downstairs—he's going to get coal in for the Aga.' Belinda sat down with a bump on the end of the bed, and Amy winced as a pain shot through her still aching head.

'Downstairs?' she asked stupidly.

'Yes—isn't he brilliant? He called the college to let me know you were ill, and offered to collect me and bring me home when his surgery finished. And—well, he did, and here I am.'

They heard the back door being opened and then the unmistakable sound of coke being shovelled into the coal bucket. Amy's hazy thoughts meandered back to the morning and the doctor's gentle examination of baby Jonathan. His long fingers had so tenderly travelled over the small body, it seemed all wrong that those same hands should now be grappling with the Kincaid fuel supply.

'You could have done that, Belinda, it's not fair to ask a stranger.' She closed her eyes and took another sip of lemon. She really felt most peculiar, she ached right through to her bones, and even sitting up made her feel giddy.

Belinda pouted. 'Well, in the first place he's not a stranger, you work with him, and his children are at school with Jen—and anyway, he offered!' She stood up and twirled around in the tiny space at the end of the bed. She held up a hand in front of her and studied the long painted fingernails. 'Max said that hands like mine aren't made for shovelling coal.'

Amy turned her head into the pillow. Was it worth pointing out to her spoilt sister that his hands were infinitely more valuable than hers? No, she was too tired to argue; too tired even to ask Belinda to turn her pillows and straighten the sheets while she went to the bathroom.

'Go away,' she said in a weak, resigned voice. 'Offer Dr Bentley tea or a drink, there's a decent sherry or that white wine in the fridge.'

'Well, I was only trying to help—excuse me for breathing!' snapped Belinda in a sarcastic voice. A moment later she seemed to regret this. 'Oh, look, Amy—I'm sorry, I didn't mean to say that. I would like to help, truly. I really am sorry you're ill.'

She was patently sincere. That, thought Amy, was what made dealing with her younger sister so difficult. She was hard and selfish one minute, and soft and generous the next. Somehow through her pain and discomfort she brought forth a smile of sorts.

'Perhaps you'd refill these hot water bottles,' she suggested. 'I'm going to the bathroom.'

She dragged herself across the little landing as Belinda went downstairs with the bottles. Max's voice, or rather his deep resonant tones, drifted up the staircase, but she couldn't make out what he was saying.

She would have liked to have showered, but her legs felt too wobbly. Instead she filled the basin with steaming hot water, and sponged herself off from top to toe. Astonishingly, even the hot water felt cool. 'You must have a hell of a temp,' she muttered to herself, as she finished her ablutions and shuffled back to her room.

'Come on, hop in,' instructed a deep masculine voice. 'Lots more fluids for you, my girl, and plenty of sleep.'

Amy saw through startled, misty eyes that Max
Bentley was standing by her bed. The pillows had been
turned and plumped up, the sheets stretched smooth,
one bottle warmed the pillows and another bulged
beneath the turned-back clothes at the foot of the bed.
For once, all thoughts of independence left her. She put
out a hand, mutely begging for support, and he took it,
and guided her to the bed. She sank down with a sigh of
such relief that he smiled—a kind, compassionate smile.

'In,' he said firmly, and with one deft movement
whisked off her slippers and dressing gown and pushed
her gently back on to the pillows. It was done so quickly
and neatly that she had no time to feel embarrassed or
uncomfortable.

He lowered his long lean form carefully on to the side
of the bed, avoiding her aching legs and feet. He busied
himself with a glass of juice and several tablets from the
collection on the table. 'Here,' he said, after a few
moments, 'take these.' He tipped some tablets into her
hand and held a glass to her lips. 'Swallow for Max,' he
said softly, with a smile.

Amy obediently obliged, then sank back again against
the blessedly cool pillows. 'Now,' said Max, 'this is what
I propose. Jenny stays with us at the Manor for a few
days—it'll make it easier to collect and deliver her to
and from school, and also perhaps keep her free from
infection.' Amy nodded, and immediately wished she
hadn't, as darting pains assaulted her head.

'Thank you,' she whispered, knowing the idea was
sensible, though wishing there were other possibilities.
She felt an absolute wimp, lying around and letting the
forceful doctor take over, but she could see no practical
alternative. Jenny, sensible little girl though she was,
needed adult help and supervision, and, though in

theory Belinda should supply this, in practice her help wasn't dependable.

On the mushy outer borders of her feverish mind, Amy knew that accepting the doctor's offer was best for Jenny, and at least her little sister was giving in return; Rose depended on her at school. It was some small comfort. And of course, the doctor was fascinated by Belinda, as so many men had been before him. Helping the Kincaid sisters, if it meant helping and seeing more of Belinda, was probably reward enough for him.

Drowsily, Amy sank back on to her pillows. I must just get better as soon as possible, she thought, and be glad that Max Bentley fancies Belinda enough to put himself out to help, though it's kind of him, he's such a busy man.

'You're very kind,' she muttered softly, as the doctor tipped the glass against her lips yet again.

'We need you at the Clinic,' he replied, and his grey eyes gleamed brilliantly as they met Amy's clouded green ones for a moment. 'And both your sisters need you—you're their rock.'

He stood up and bent over her and stroked a strand of hair away from her forehead. 'Go to sleep now,' he whispered. He leaned closer, and his finger trailed down her hot cheek. 'Don't worry, I'll look after everything.'

The thought was infinitely comforting. Amy sighed with relief and fell asleep before he reached the bottom of the stairs.

For five days she remained in bed, amazed to find that she was willing to do so. Her temperature refused to come down in spite of the medication and the gallons of fluid that she consumed, and she still ached abominably.

Belinda excelled herself in giving her version of tender loving care, and was so genuinely willing and cheerful that Amy put up with her clumsiness without complaining. It was astonishing, she mused one morning, that someone as slender and ethereal-looking as her pretty sister could be so ham-fisted, and, for that matter, footed!

She would belt up the narrow staircase two at a time, lift the latch noisily on the old wooden-panelled door, and almost fall into the bedroom. Her bedmaking was painful for a trained nurse to watch, and Amy usually went to the bathroom while Belinda wrestled with sheets and blankets.

Mrs Carter was the exact opposite, quiet and efficient. She called in most afternoons, bringing a casserole or something equally delectable for Amy's and Belinda's supper. After a couple of days Jenny came in with her, though, obeying Dr Bentley's instructions, she just stood inside the doorway of Amy's bedroom and blew her a kiss.

She waved a tiny bunch of brown leaves and bright red berries at Amy. 'I picked these in the garden,' she said, 'just for you. I'll put them in a vase and Mrs Carter will put them on your dressing-table.'

Her dear little face was bright with the cold.

'How are you, darling?' croaked Amy. 'Do you like being at the Manor?'

'It's lovely! I like being with Rose and Harry, and Dr Bentley's very kind, but I do miss you. I want to come home as soon as you're better. That won't be long, will it?' Jenny finished wistfully.

'Not very long, love, and we'll have a special celebration party then; you can invite Rose and Harry as a thank-you for having you.'

'That'd be brilliant, and could Mrs Carter and Dr Bentley come too? They've been so nice to me, and I wouldn't like them to feel left out.'

'Anyone you want can come,' said Amy, blowing her nose hard, and thinking, as she had on other occasions, what a kind little girl Jenny was, and wise beyond her years.

Her other regular visitor was Max Bentley himself. Mostly he called in on his way back from St Anne's and, after enquiring how she was feeling, launched into interesting bits of gossip pertaining to the Medical Centre, or Clinic, as it was increasingly being called.

He always looked the way he had on the first occasion that she had met him, dressed in a dark grey suit, sparkling shirt, white or discreetly striped with blue or cinnamon, and an understated silk tie.

'The Man in Grey,' Amy had facetiously labelled him. It was therefore quite a surprise when he appeared one morning just after Belinda had wreaked her usual havoc in the bedroom, and Amy was surreptitiously repairing the damage.

He had come up the stairs so quietly that she hadn't heard him. His deep, gravelly voice alerted her with a jerk to his presence.

'What the hell do you think you're doing?' he asked from the doorway.

'I'm—I'm—just—just. . .' Amy turned and faced him, and saw at once that this was not a usual visit. In the first place, it was the wrong time of day. It was morning, a bright, cold morning, with a pale disc of a sun floating in a pale blue sky. In the second place, she noted with astonishment, the doctor was not wearing a grey suit and highly polished black Oxfords, but a blue and red track-suit and trainers.

Amy gaped at this apparition, then collapsed on to the bed, helpless with laughter. Laughter punctuated a moment later by a paroxysm of coughing that was painful and noisy.

Between coughs and gulping laughter, she tried to
explain. 'I'm s-sorry,' she stammered. 'I must seem
rude—it's just that you look so different.' The lengthy
speech took its toll, and she coughed again, long and
painfully. When she had finished coughing, she finished
her speech. 'I can't believe you're going to the Clinic
looking like that,' she said on a splutter.

Max was smiling now, and had moved over to the
bed, swung her legs round until she was horizontal, and
pulled the blankets up over her feverish form.

'I'm not going to the Clinic,' he explained, 'because
it's Saturday, and I've no surgery, and I'm not even on
call.'

Amy smiled at him. She still felt disorientated and
couldn't believe it was the weekend already.

'It's nice to see you,' she said, 'in something other
than a beautifully tailored grey suit.'

'Well, if I'd known you felt that way about it, I'd
have shed my professional image sooner,' he told her
with a wide, friendly smile.

'Would you like coffee or something?' asked Amy, at
a loss to know quite how to deal with this relaxed,
easygoing man. Before he could answer she became
aware that the house was silent except for their voices.
'Where's Belinda?' she asked.

'Caught the bus into Castleminster, I hope,' replied
Max, his voice very calm and deep.

'Castleminster?' she queried.

'There's some sort of student rally on, so I understand. She was very keen to go. I've offered to invalid-
sit, if that's all right with you.'

'Oh, I am sorry. You don't have to stay, you know.
I'll be quite all right by myself.'

'Well, I didn't know you'd find an hour or two in my
company quite so devastating. But I don't think Belinda

would have gone had I not offered to stay. She's taking her duties looking after you very seriously.'

'I didn't mean I didn't want. . .oh dear, what I mean is, you'll find it dull with. . .' Amy was about to say 'without Belinda', but changed her mind. He would not, she thought, like her to refer to his interest in her sister, and he was used to exercising control, so he could probably take her absence in his stride.

What was really surprising was that Belinda had apparently left the house happily, knowing Max was there. She must be very sure of him to have gone off, even for a few hours. Of course, she might be deliberately playing it cool, to excite his interest further. But he won't buy that, Amy thought, and was overcome with embarrassment, not sure if she had spoken her thoughts out loud.

She covered her confusion with another coughing fit, and Max was instantly at the side of the bed, offering her a drink.

'That cough's still very troublesome, Amy. Are you taking all your medication as prescribed?'

'Of course I am. I wouldn't dream of not doing so after all the trouble everyone went to when I collapsed the other day,' she assured him.

'Hm, you're expectorating well; what you probably need now is a good old-fashioned soothing syrup, something like linctus pholcodeine. Will you be all right for half an hour if I pop along to the nearest chemist to collect some? I believe there's one on the outskirts of town. I'll write up a scrip and square it with Elliot Grey, I'm sure he won't mind, even though he's your GP.'

'Well, yes, I'll be fine, but it isn't fair on you having to work on your day off. Can't it wait till Monday?'

'My dear Amy, I wouldn't suggest leaving you, even

for a short while, if I thought you could wait till
Monday. I think you need a palliative right now.'

'Well, who am I to argue?'

'Exactly,' he said, and, bending, brushed a feather-
light kiss across her forehead, before going quietly
downstairs.

Amy lay stiffly on her bed listening to the doctor
locking up the back door and going out through the
front.

Was she delirious? she wondered. Had she imagined
that his lips had brushed across her hot forehead? No, it
had definitely happened, but why—why should his
practical, and, if the truth be acknowledged, his vested
interest in her recovery persuade him to do that? He
didn't have to impress her further with his willingness
to help the Kincaids. He didn't have to pretend that his
motives were other than promoting his interest in a
ménage that contained both Belinda and Jenny. So why
gild the gingerbread?

Lulled into a sense of security in the knowledge that
Max would be back, she fell asleep before reaching any
conclusions in the matter.

When she woke, it was to find that the pale blue
winter sky had clouded over and was gunmetal grey,
and the light was dim. Max was sitting in the small
basket chair that just fitted the tiny space between her
bed and dressing-table. He seemed to overflow the cane
back, and it creaked as he leaned towards her. An
aromatic scent rose from the staircase.

Amy sniffed automatically.

'Onion soup,' Max told her. 'Made to a recipe that I
inherited from my maternal grandmother. She was part
Hungarian. You'd have liked her, Amy, and she would
have loved you.'

'I can't think why,' said Amy.

Max didn't seem surprised by her comment. 'Because you're you, because you don't dissemble. You're natural and practical and loving.'

'Gosh, am I really?'

'Really,' he said, and gave a sort of subdued bellow of laughter.

Amy suddenly realised she was feeling much better. Her thumping headache had gone, and though she still ached all over it was a less acute ache than that which she had previously endured.

She pushed herself up in the bed. 'I feel better,' she said triumphantly, 'much better.'

Max rose from his chair and it creaked alarmingly. 'Good. What about risking a trip downstairs? It's quiet, lunch is ready, and I'm here to lend a hand!'

'I must go to the bathroom first,' said Amy. 'And Dr Grey said I must wait till he gives the go-ahead for me to venture downstairs.'

'Ah, yes. Well, I met Elliot when I was on my way to collect your medication. He's of the opinion that you're in good hands,' Max showed his hands palms uppermost, 'and has more or less passed you over into my care. He, of course, knows we work together, and appreciates my concern.'

For a moment Amy's happiness was dented. Did Dr Grey know, she wondered, that Max had the interests of his daughter Rose at heart, and that little Jenny played such a large part in her day-to-day happiness? And did he know that Belinda, in all her radiant and youthful beauty, had caught Max Bentley's eye, and that she, Amy, was the catalyst for both? It was most unlikely.

'Come on, my dear, let me help you on with your dressing-gown,' Max was saying, holding up the ancient blue woollen garment for Amy to slip into. He wrapped the gown round her as if it was something special and valuable. 'There,' he said, in a comforting way. 'You're as snug as a bug in a rug. Now hop into the bathroom, and I'll be ready to take you down.'

Amy thought she would never forget that first trip downstairs following her attack of flu. Max had ended up by carrying her, since her legs had collapsed halfway down the short staircase. He deposited her on the sofa and gently tucked a rug around her before disappearing into the tiny kitchen.

When he came out, he was carrying a tray laden with a steaming dish of soup and a small, napkin-lined basket filled with hot French bread. Amy's appetite, which had been non-existent for days, returned, and she tucked into the feast with a gusto that encouraged her to tackle two bowls of soup.

Max sat at the table nearby and kept pace with her. 'I told you it would be good,' he said, unable to conceal his delight in her enjoyment of the food. 'And for dessert we have,' he waved his arms in the manner of a magician, 'lemon sorbet and vanilla ice-cream, nourishing but clean to the palate.'

'But I don't think. . .'

'You'll manage it,' he said, and his voice was firm and assured. 'Because I want you to.' He bent over her and put a forefinger beneath her chin. 'You'll do it for me, love, won't you?'

Amy nodded, and he brought the dessert, served in a pretty cut glass dish. Delicately he lifted a spoonful of sorbet to her lips. 'There,' he said softly as she opened her mouth and swallowed the tangy offering. 'that wasn't too bad, was it?'

Amy shook her head. 'No,' she murmured, 'it was lovely.'

When they had finished lunch, Max took away the dishes and washed them up. He returned to the sitting-room and added more logs to the fire. 'Now,' he suggested, 'what about some music? I see you're a lover of the cello!'

Amy nodded.

'So am I,' he said. 'What about Pablo Casals playing the César Franck Sonata? I see you've got that in your collection.'

'Lovely,' she replied, and let herself drift off into sleep to the delicious deep throbbing tones conjured up by Casals' fingers on the cello strings.

CHAPTER SIX

THE memory of that magical afternoon lingered with Amy over the next few days, as she gradually gained strength. Apple logs—surplus from the Manor House gardens, Max had explained, from trees that had fallen in the autumn gales—burned aromatically in the old-fashioned brick fireplace. The throbbing cello music, and Max, at first seated in an armchair opposite the sofa, but at some point moving to sit on the fireside rug with his back resting against the sofa, altered the whole afternoon. It became unreal, mystical.

Amy longed to stretch out a hand and smooth the thick grey-black hair. She resisted, rather shocked by her desire to touch this handsome, kindly man who had, for whatever motive, come to the aid of the Kincaid sisters. He might be enamoured of Belinda and grateful for Jenny's help with Rose, but he had shown an overall interest in their welfare, and a generous willingness to be a good neighbour. She must not do anything to spoil his friendly concern.

For nearly a week, Amy spent much of each day down in the sitting-room. 'Reclining on the sofa,' she said jokingly to Max when he called in one afternoon on his way home from the Clinic, 'like a Victorian miss with the vapours.'

'I can't imagine you giving way to any such feminine weakness,' he said with a laugh. 'You're much too tough and modern—only something as advanced as the latest derivation of the flu bug could lay you low.'

She took it as a compliment of sorts, though half regretting his description of 'tough', which seemed to imply lack of femininity.

Max seated himself in the chair at the other side of the fireplace, as had become his habit on his regular visits. He had already performed what had also become a habit, the pouring of a fresh glass of lemonade for Amy, which he then encouraged her to drink while he stood by the sofa looking down on her.

On one occasion Amy had protested, 'But I've only just finished a glass!'

'No matter,' Max had replied. 'At least I know for sure that you've had some of your quota of fluids if I see you drink it.'

She had not objected after that, and indeed she welcomed his attention. It was this attention to small detail for her own and her sisters' comfort that she found so endearing and reassuring.

On this particular evening he came into the tiny hall, brushing flakes of snow from his suede car coat.

'It's bitterly cold out,' he said, standing in front of the fire to warm his hands. After a moment he turned to the tray on the small side table where the usual jug full of fruit juice resided. Her glass was full. 'Ah, you've beaten me to it.'

'Yes, for once I have, Max. Truly I've only just finished a glass—this is a fresh one.'

'All right, my love, I believe you.'

The endearment was said in his usual tone of voice, and Amy realised that there was no special significance in the remark, but her heart bounded with pleasure just the same.

Max sat down in what had become regarded as his armchair. He steepled his fingers and rested his chin on them. His grey eyes surveyed her calmly yet compassionately.

He said in his deep voice, 'Elliot Grey tells me you're plaguing him to get back to work!'

'Well, yes, I'm sure I'm fit enough. It's been ten days, Max.'

'Give it a bit longer and I'm sure Elliot will let you return,' he said quietly. 'Your car should be ready by then, and in reasonably good nick.'

'But what's happened to it—it's not badly damaged, is it?' she asked anxiously. 'It's been such a good friend.'

Max smiled at her, obviously amused by her turn of phrase. He said reassuringly, 'Someone gave it a knock when it was in the Clinic car park—nothing too serious. It was covered by the general insurance that we carry. A bloke came along, a patient, a mechanic interested in the earlier Fiats, and he's fixing it. He assures me it'll go like a bomb when he's finished dealing with it.'

'When will it be ready?' asked Amy.

'By the middle of next week. I'll see it's delivered by Wednesday in time for you to start work Thursday. How does that grab you?'

'That's great,' she smiled. 'I can't wait to get back!'

'Well, I'm sure everyone at the Clinic will be pleased to see you,' said Max, in what Amy thought was a rather subdued tone. 'But don't be surprised if you feel exhausted after your first duty.'

'Oh, no, of course I won't.' Amy felt she should say more—she wanted to say more. She wanted to thank him for all he had done since she became ill, but somehow the words wouldn't come.

He levered his long, lean body from the low armchair and stood looking down at her, his grey eyes looking soft, gentle, almost blue in the lamplight.

'Amy,' he crouched down beside the sofa, 'I. . .'

The front door opened with a crash and Belinda exploded into the sitting-room. She looked like a picture from an old-fashioned Christmas card. A few snow-flecked curls escaped from beneath a velvet cap, her blue eyes sparkled, a long, elegant if shabby black cloak that she'd picked up at Oxfam on one of her rare economy drives almost swept the floor.

She looked utterly radiant. Max rose to his feet and stared at her, a strange expression on his face. He's overwhelmed with love and admiraton, thought Amy, and he's quite forgotten whatever it was that he was about to say to me.

'Hi,' said Belinda cheerfully. 'Isn't it lovely—the snow? We may have a white Christmas for once. Do you think we will, Max?' She turned her shining blue eyes on him, with a little girl face, full of expectancy.

'Well,' his voice sounded even deeper, throatier than usual, 'I suppose it's possible, though it's a bit early to say yet, as we're not far into November.'

'Wouldn't it be marvellous, though, if we did? The Green,' Belinda waved her hand towards the darkened window that looked over the wide expanse of grass that was the centre of the village, 'would look wonderful, and the Downs aren't far away. We could go sledging, couldn't we?'

'I dare say we could,' said Max on a laugh.

Amy fought to hide her chagrin. He was behaving just as any other besotted male behaved when faced with an ebullient and happy Belinda. She had thought he might be capable of some restraint, but obviously she was wrong. She studied his face. The long, lean contours looked serious enough, but his mouth was curled up into a delicious smile, and his eyes were bright with adulation and anticipation.

'We have a sledge, haven't we, Amy!' said Belinda,

eyes sparkling, cheeks glowing. 'It needs repairing, though. Perhaps you, Max, or your Mr Carter could do that.'

'Belinda, you mustn't expect Max or his gardener to do any more.' Amy was shocked by Belinda's forthrightness. 'I'm sorry,' she said to Max, thinking that even though he was besotted with her sister he would resent being taken for granted.

'Why?' he asked. 'I'd be delighted to fix the sledge, or have it fixed, I can't imagine anything better than sliding down the snow-covered hills, and I'm sure the children would love it.' He looked at Amy in a puzzled, almost irritated fashion, as if it was she and not Belinda who was being troublesome.

Amy picked up the knitting she had abandoned when Max arrived, and bent her head over it to hide the hurt in her eyes.

Her peace was shattered, and the pain she felt in the region of her heart was almost physical, as if something was breaking within her. Her practical, matter-of-fact mind told her there was no such thing as a broken heart, that just didn't happen in real life. Hearts were tough, muscular organs, which could survive an astonishing amount of damage, and hers was as tough as they come. Hadn't the good doctor himself described her as such?

She forced herself to remain cheerful for the short while that Max remained, and even joined in the bantering conversation that he and Belinda exchanged. She managed a bright 'goodnight' when he left, and told herself it was because she didn't want to see him hurt that she was disturbed by his interest in Belinda.

Only later that night did Amy admit to the true reason for her pain and distress where Max was concerned. She could no longer make light of it, or make facetious jokes at her own expense, about broken hearts, even to herself. She was in love with the man—there was no doubt about it.

Until now she had admired him, both as a professional and as a man. She had been grateful to him for being a good friend and neighbour, and had acknowledged his animal magnetism, his masculine charisma. Mildly, she had resented his attraction to Belinda, but until this moment she had rejected her feelings for what they were, those of a woman deeply in love.

Common sense told her she hadn't a hope in hell of Max returning her love. He was infatuated with Belinda, and if he survived that, or succeeded in taming her, the most she herself could expect was a continuing friendship with him. So be it, she decided, tossing restlessly in her bed, I'll settle for being the world's best sister-in-law.

It was as well that she was now much improved and on the road to recovery from the flu bug, for when she woke she felt and looked exhausted and hollow-eyed. Had they seen her at breakfast that morning, neither of the medical men interested in her welfare would have given her a clean bill of health for a few days' hence.

Amy grappled with her conscience, using every ounce of her practical approach to life to come to terms with the turmoil within her. When the time came for her to return to work, she was sure she would have everything under control, and be able to greet Max Bentley in a friendly but not too fulsome manner.

She would thank him properly, too, for all that he had done for the Kincaid family, and quietly resume control of the Doll's House.

No one, she was convinced, was hurt or in any way affected by her private heart-searching and innermost emotions. No one except herself was aware of her feelings for Max. Life could continue as it had before she had so ignominiously collapsed at the Clinic.

She felt happier once she had reached these high-minded conclusions, and resolved to remain so.

Her car was delivered the day before she was due on duty. The mechanic who had worked on it knocked at the cottage door to hand over the keys.

'I'm Wayne Thorogood,' he explained when she opened the door. 'Returning that little beauty to Miss Amy Kincaid.' He pointed to the kerb where there stood a shiny red Fiat.

'I'm Amy Kincaid,' said Amy, holding out her hand for the key. She stared at the car. 'Gosh, it looks almost new!'

'Well, it's practically had a re-spray. As the doc said, might as well make a job of it as I was patching up the latest dent, and tuning up the engine.'

'I didn't know the insurance would cover all that.' The mechanic opened his mouth to say something, but Amy forestalled him by asking why he was so interested in Fiats. 'It isn't as if they have the sort of charm that goes with a Mini,' she said.

It turned out that Wayne had done his training in a garage that specialised in Fiats, and simply enjoyed bringing them up to scratch. He would have enlarged upon this, but at that moment a van driven by one of his workmates drew up to collect him.

'I hope she goes all right for you, miss,' said Wayne as he got into the other vehicle. 'She's going as sweet as a nut at the moment.'

Amy decided to try the car out as she was starting work the next day. Muffled up in a thick jacket, as the car heater was a bit temperamental, fur gloves and hat, she set off through the gloom of the November afternoon. At least the snow of the previous week had vanished, and though it was cold, it wasn't freezing.

After only a few minutes she realised how much better the engine was turning over. It was a joy to drive. She sailed up the hill outside the village, instead of crawling with the engine grinding unhappily. She switched on the heater, and to her amazement lovely warm air belted out of the vents. It began to rain as she reached the summit of the hill, and she decided to take the narrow lane out of the valley that led back round the north side of the village.

'You're a little beauty,' she said to the car, patting the dashboard. 'I reckon Wayne Thorogood has done us proud.'

The rain was now sheeting down, and the afternoon light was failing fast, though it was only just after four. Amy switched on her lights and slowed down as she reached the foot of the hill, signalling that she was about to turn left into Bottom Lane. There was a sharp bend ahead of her just after the turning, rising steeply up the next hill, going towards Castleminster.

At that moment, as she was about to turn, a low-slung, sporty-looking car, which must have been doing at least seventy, screeched round the bend towards her.

It wasn't going to make it, she realised.

She slammed on the brakes and slewed into the hedge.

She jerked round in her seat to watch with horror as the car hit the verge side-on and rolled over and over.

Amy wasn't sure how long she sat with the rain beating down on the roof of the Fiat after the crash. It was probably only seconds, but it could have been five minutes or more before she began to function. Her first conscious thought was to examine her own situation. She had veered into the hedge. By the headlights she could see that her car was at a bit of an angle on the

grass verge, but not alarmingly so. Because she had
braked suddenly she had been restrained by her seat-
belt, and she was now aware that her chest and waist
felt sore, where the belt had pulled tight. Otherwise, she
was fine.

Carefully she unfastened her belt and opened the
door. The dark sky and driving rain made visibility
poor. She collected a torch from the glove compartment
and crossed the road to where the upturned car lay. It
was uncannily quiet, apart from the rain splashing down
and occasional gusts of wind. Certainly there was no
other vehicle to be heard coming either from the village
or from Castleminster.

Oddly enough, she felt very calm and controlled. She
didn't know what she would find when she reached the
car, but she was prepared for anything. It was years
since she had worked in Casualty, and then it was as a
student, but automatically she reacted as she might
have done then, with a suppressed alertness, fuelled by
adrenalin and the knowledge that she must work fast
but carefully. She psyched herself up for whatever she
might find as she made her diagonal walk across the
road.

The car had come to rest upside down, impaled on
something that had stoved in the front of the wind-
screen. The hot metal contracted with little pinging
sounds as the cold needles of rain beat down on the
underside of the vehicle.

Amy crouched down and looked through the window
on the driver's side. The sight that met her eyes was
horrific. The driver, obviously not wearing a seatbelt,
had shot forward, and was hard against the steering
wheel. His face was pressed into the laminated wind-
screen, which had buckled and cracked, but was still in

one piece. His forehead was smashed and bleeding, and partly stoved in.

Amy thought he was probably dead; his head was at a strange angle, he must have hit the roof as the car turned over, and then fallen forward. The door wouldn't budge, so she reached in through the side window, carefully avoiding some spiky bits of broken glass, and tried to take his temporal pulse. There was nothing to be felt, but that might be on account of his head injuries, and not because he was dead. Not that there was anything she could do for him unaided. She'd better look at the passenger.

It was then that Amy noticed the keys hanging from the ignition. The engine had stopped, probably when the car first started to turn over, but she remembered hearing that one should switch off the ignition in a damaged car. She switched it off and pocketed the key, straightened up and took a few deep breaths, mentally ticking off what she should do next. It was at that moment that she became aware of another vehicle slowing up some twenty yards past the overturned car.

Relief at help arriving was almost her undoing. She began to shake, and then calling on all her reserves and training, pulled herself together. Probably the driver of the newly arrived car would be far more shocked than she, since so many people outside the medical and nursing professions had never seen maimed or dead bodies. She must be strong and take charge.

The dark was like night now, and the driving rain obscured all but the vaguest outlines of a large car and then the driver, as he stepped out of the vehicle.

The driver ran with long strides towards her, as she called, 'Over here!' as if he hadn't noticed her car, or the overturned car when he came round the bend.

'Amy—my God, are you all right?' called a deep

voice, staccato with fear, and Max, suddenly visible a
few feet away, was there in front of her.

He grabbed her by the shoulders. 'My dear, dear
girl,' he said shakily.

'Max?' Amy gabbled in amazement. 'Oh, Max—you!
I can't believe it!'

He pulled her to him and put his arms round her, but
briefly. 'Tell me,' he said as she took great gulping
breaths against his chest, 'what happened?' Even as he
spoke, he was edging them both towards the wrecked
car.

Yet again she pulled herself together and gave Max a
sensible account of what had happened and what she
had already discovered.

'And you think the driver's dead?'

Amy nodded. 'Well, he's at least deeply unconscious,
but I haven't had time to look at the passenger.'

They had reached the car and went straight to the
passenger window. Max had a torch with him which he
shone between the jagged broken glass. A young woman
with blood trickling down her forehead was jammed
upside down against the roof. Her seatbelt was intact.
Her face looked purplish and congested in the
torchlight.

'Fetch my bag, and then use the car phone to get
emergency services, ambulance first, then police and
fire,' Max said tersely. 'And there's a red and white
flasher lamp. Stick that on the roof.'

Amy swallowed, muttered that she understood, then
ran back to the Range Rover, and within a second was
back again with the medical bag.

Max had by now opened the door of the upside-down
car and was taking the passenger's radial pulse.

'Thready,' he said, 'poor volume—we haven't much
time. Go and phone.'

It seemed hours before the ambulance arrived, although it wasn't. They worked frantically to free the passenger. Max supported the slight form, while Amy released her seatbelt, but easing her out of the unnatural position she was in was difficult, virtually impossible. Max did what he could, putting clean dressings over her head and facial injuries after testing her pupils for reaction.

'Poor girl,' he said softly. 'She almost certainly has a depressed compound skull fracture, and, most worrying of all, spinal damage. We mustn't move her any more till help comes. It's going to be one hell of a job, and she's got leg injuries too, I think. Here, shine the torch down.'

He continued to support the girl while Amy directed the light on to the trapped legs and bent to examine them as best she could.

She straightened up, her face pale and set. 'They're partly trapped beneath the dashboard—it's been bashed in by something, the old milestone, I think. Her right leg's badly damaged, looks like a possible comminuted fracture of tib and fib,' she said grimly. 'We ought to try covering it, but you've nothing else suitable left in your case.' They stared at each other for a moment, then Amy exclaimed, 'Of course, my first aid box! I won't be a minute.' She ran across the road to her beleaguered car.

She was scrabbling beneath the passenger seat where she stowed the kit, when she heard a tractor rumbling along Bottom Lane. Its powerful headlights were blazing, and as it came to a halt where the lane joined the B-road into Castleminster, they lit up the scene of the accident, like a stage. Even the little Fiat was bathed obliquely in light.

The driver slid back the window of his cab, and saw Amy at once.

'Bloody 'ell!' he said in a shocked voice. 'What's happened here, then?' and in a gentler tone he asked, 'Are you all right?'

Later Amy knew she had never thought so fast or instinctively before.

'Look, I'm a nurse. There are two badly injured people over there, but a doctor's with them. The emergency people have been alerted and will be here soon. Can you leave your tractor there with the lights on, and go up the road that way,' she pointed towards Castleminster, 'and stop any other vehicle coming round the bend? We don't want the road blocked when they get here.'

The man seemed to understand at once.

'Right, will do,' he said, and climbed down from his cab.

Amy found the first aid kit, which had slid into the back of the car, and rushed back with it to Max. His face, she noted, in spite of her preoccupation with the trapped passenger, was showing signs of strain. In order to hold the injured girl in the best position, he was crouching uncomfortably by the car, as he supported her. It didn't, however, stop him being sharp with Amy as she appeared beside him.

'You've taken your time,' he muttered through tight lips, then immediately apologised. 'Sorry,' he said, and sounded as if he meant it.

She was at first shocked by his brusqueness, but immediately accepted his apology.

'It's all right,' she said. 'I understand.' Instinctively she knew that he wanted to do more for the injured people, and was frustrated because he couldn't. He must also be numb with shock and cold, she thought, as

she secured a clean but by no means perfect dressing
loosely over the messy injury on the girl's lower leg. She
wished she could take over for him even for a few
minutes, but knew that supporting an inert body in that
position was beyond her strength.

'A tractor's just arrived,' she told Max, knowing the
news would cheer him. 'The driver's going to stop
vehicles coming down the road on this side for the
moment, and he's leaving his lights on, which might be
a help.'

'That was good thinking,' Max agreed, somehow
raising the semblance of a smile, and Amy knew he
realised it was she who had come up with the idea, and
was pleased with his approval.

She had brought a rug with her from the car, and this
she now placed carefully over the recumbent form of the
injured girl.

'There's morphine in my bag,' said Max. 'Draw up
two milligrams and give an intramuscular in the front
of her thigh. I think you can reach there.'

Amy had just finished giving the injection when they
heard the sound of a siren, and, soon after, an ambulance appeared and drew up beside them. Behind the
ambulance came a police car, and a little later, a fire
brigade vehicle.

Amy had supposed the fire brigade was necessary in
case the damaged car caught fire, but she saw now that
their help was to be used in another context. Max, who
had been relieved of supporting the young woman by
the ambulance men, was discussing the possibility of
removing the rear door of the sports car with the senior
brigade officer. This would allow the removal of the
passenger, without further injury.

Waiting to be allowed to go home, giving her statement to the police and then being asked to repeat it to a

more senior officer who arrived on the scene, was tedious
and exhausting. Surplus to requirements, with all the
skilled emergency personnel around, Amy was growing
colder and more uncomfortable by the minute.

Max was still involved with the fire and ambulance
officers. The rear door had been wrenched off the car
and the patient was slowly being removed, under his
supervision.

It was a shock to learn that the police would not
allow Amy to remove her car until a special unit had
arrived and examined the area. When they came, they
looked at her tyres and took measurements from the
other side of the road, at all sorts of angles.

'But I told you,' Amy said crossly to the senior officer,
'I wasn't involved at all in what happened. I simply
pulled off the road because I thought the sports car was
going to hit me.'

'Yes, miss,' said the officer soothingly. 'It's only
routine.'

Amy fumed, and wanted to tell him not to be so
patronising. The tractor driver, who had been relieved
of his watching brief on the traffic, was sympathetic, but
he could only say what he had found when he arrived
on the scene, and not what had happened before he
arrived.

When at last Max joined her, having seen both
casualties into the ambulance, she was still fuming, but
brought her anger under control when she saw how
tired he was.

'What are their chances?' she asked, as they watched
the ambulance draw away.

'The young woman might make it, but I'm sure the
driver will be classed DOA.'

A policeman came up to Amy at that point and told

her she could drive her car away, but might be needed to sign her statement at the station the following day.

'Why, is there a problem?' asked Max sharply.

'Oh no, sir, it's just routine,' replied the policeman.

At last they were on their way home, Amy's little Fiat bowling along behind the rugged Range Rover.

'Well, your insides seem none the worse for wear,' she told her four-wheeled steed, patting the steering wheel affectionately. 'I do hope your brush with the hedge hasn't spoilt your beautiful new paintwork.'

She felt rather light-headed with relief now that the horrific incident was behind her. Max's words of appreciation as he handed her into her car rang in her ears. 'You were splendid, Amy,' he had said, giving her a tired but warm smile. 'Calm and professional, and very reassuring. Intelligent too, the way you organised the tractor driver. You're a very special person.' His grey eyes had gleamed as they stared straight into hers, and his mobile mouth had softened as he bent towards her.

Would he have kissed her, she wondered later, if circumstances had been different, or had her imagination been working overtime? By the time they reached the village, collected Jenny from the Manor House, where she was still going after school, and given Mrs Carter a guarded account of the accident, Amy was sure he had simply been kind and generous in his praise. He was only expressing his professional appreciation of the part she had played in the afternoon's disaster.

Max's concern prompted him to suggest that Amy delay her return to the clinic by another day, after the trauma of the accident, but Amy wouldn't hear of it. More than ever she wanted to get back to work and establish a routine that included Dr Bentley as a colleague, and a good friend, but nothing more.

She went to bed that night tired, but in a strange way exhilarated by the events of the day. Glad she had been able to rise to the occasion, desperately sorry for the two young people involved in the drama, and especially the young woman, but restored in confidence in herself and her future relations with Max.

CHAPTER SEVEN

THE most significant thing about Amy's return to work the following day was the passing, on her way to St Anne's, of the upturned sports car, a grim reminder of the accident.

The car was resting on the old-fashioned granite milestone, with the legend, '4 MILES TO CASTLE-MINSTER' carved on it. It was the milestone that had brought the speeding vehicle to a sudden halt yesterday afternoon. Beside the car was a police notice saying, 'DO NOT REMOVE.' Quite why this was so, Amy couldn't decide. Presumably something to do with further enquiries into the accident.

This reminded her that she might yet have to go to the police station to sign her statement—a thought that caused butterflies in her stomach for a few minutes, until she comforted herself with the knowledge that she had nothing to fear. She had Max's reassurance that all would be well, and his support gave her confidence. She also remembered, with a shiver of pleasure, the tone of his voice when he had arrived at the scene of the accident and taken her, albeit briefly, into his arms.

Resolutely she squashed this exquisite memory, reminding herself of her determination to think of Max Bentley as a friend, and possible future relative, but nothing more where she was concerned.

Her resolve nearly crumpled, though, when, as she was parking her car— still shiny bright and unscratched in spite of yesterday's head-on meeting with the hedge— Max arrived. He tooted at her to wait, and gave her a

89

heart-stopping smile as he drew up into his parking
space.

'Hello, Amy,' he said, and his deep warm voice
invested her name with seductive overtones. Surely no
one had ever made her short, no-nonsense name sound
like that?

'Hi,' she replied, trying to neutralise his warmth with
cool friendliness. 'Lovely morning, but rather chilly.'

Max frowned, clearly surprised by the manner of her
response. 'Yes,' he looked vaguely around him as if to
confirm or deny her remark. 'Yes, it is cold, but nice
and dry, rather different from yesterday.' He smiled at
her again in an encouraging fashion, as if he wanted to
remind her about the events of the dark, wet afternoon
when they had worked closely together.

For some reason that she herself couldn't fathom, his
reminder only served to make her more determined to
put their relationship on to a casual, laid-back basis.
Perhaps she instinctively knew, that if she didn't make
a stand now against his persuasive charm and her self-
acknowledged love, she never would.

Deliberately she misunderstood him. 'Yes, it was
pretty unpleasant, wasn't it, working in the rain and the
dark? I wonder how that poor woman is doing—you
haven't heard, I suppose?'

Whatever he was now thinking about her attitude to
him, Max had recovered his usual sophisticated veneer,
and replied in a flat voice, 'I rang ICU this morning,
but got the expected spiel about the patient being
comfortable. I plan to ring later, when there's a medico
I know on duty who might be more forthcoming.'

'Good. You'll let me know, won't you?'

'Of course.'

They were walking side by side now, towards the
Clinic entrance. Max took her arm as they reached the

door. 'Amy, are you sure you're all right?' he asked, the warmth back in his voice again.

She knew she must ignore the concern in his grey eyes, and the tone of his voice; she must not read anything more into them. They were only evidence of his interest in her welfare as a colleague and the sister of the girl with whom he was in love, and whom he would persuade, if he had not already done so, to love him in return.

She must ignore the masculine magnetism of this man for Belinda's sake. Belinda, who might behave casually and seem only to want to flirt with this calm, distinguished man, but who, Amy was sure this time, in spite of her usual frivolous way with men, looked upon Max as more than a passing fancy. How could it be otherwise, she reasoned, if a man like the doctor made it plain that he was attracted to her?

Gently Amy shook herself free from his hand and the electric pulses that his touch was sending in quivering waves along her nervous system. 'I'm fine.' She was pleased with her firm voice. 'I just can't wait to get stuck into work!'

Before he could do so, she put her finger on the bell and heard it ringing shrilly in the passageway. A moment later the door was opened, and she was greeted with a cry of delight from Julie, another one of the receptionists. 'Oh, it is nice to see you!' she said, and half spoilt it by adding, 'We're not up to full strength yet, and every pair of hands is needed.' She clapped a hand over her mouth, realising what she had said.

Amy reassured her. She didn't mind, it was nice to be missed for whatever reason. A rather subdued Julie went on to tell Max that there had been several calls for him. On receipt of this information, he excused himself

to both women, and went through to the main reception
desk.

Within a few minutes of reporting to manager Janet
Brown, and being welcomed back by her and other
people coming on duty, Amy received her list of chores
for the day. In the morning, she was on general escort
duties from reception, which might or might not involve
her in staying with a patient who was being examined;
in the afternoon, she was seconded to Dr Bentley's chest
clinic.

She nearly betrayed herself on hearing this. She
wanted to protest and suggest that someone else cover
for her, but Janet's words stopped her.

'He seems to have taken a liking to you, Amy—
perhaps it's because you're neighbours,' explained
Janet. 'He had asked that you should do his clinic
regularly the day you went sick. Perhaps he knows
something of your nursing skills from your old training
hospital?' Amy shook her head. 'Well,' continued Janet,
'I know he's rather demanding, but he evidently likes
the way you work. And you were a hit with the patients.
Several of them have asked if you're going to be there
whenever they attend his clinic. They tend, of course, to
be long-term where chests are concerned, and more in
need of continuity.'

Amy was pleased, curious and rather overwhelmed.
'I don't understand,' she said to Janet. 'I only worked
with him for one session—he can't possibly have formed
a sensible opinion about my ability in that short time.'

'Well, he's either done that, or he has an ulterior
motive for wanting you on a regular basis.' Janet, who
was a nice, straightforward person, looked at Amy
speculatively. 'There isn't an ulterior motive, I suppose,
is there?' she asked.

'Oh, no, nothing whatsoever,' Amy assured her hurriedly, wondering whether it was another ploy by the doctor to get closer to Belinda through her. 'What could there be?'

'What indeed?' Janet smiled and turned to her desk and the usual mound of paperwork that confronted her. She lifted her head for a moment and smiled at Amy. 'I think some of the younger nurses are a bit afraid of Dr Bentley, he always looks so elegant and rather remote.'

'Well, from what I saw of him at the clinic on my first stint with him they needn't be bothered. He's a very kind and considerate doctor, marvellous with the patients, and understanding with the staff, as long as they keep their minds on their work.'

'Yes, that's rather how I read the situation. He seems a little aloof, austere perhaps to some of the staff, particularly the younger ones. But I find him friendly enough. I suppose some of our colleagues might prefer him to be even more friendly, especially off duty!'

Janet gave Amy a quirky smile, and bent her head over her work again. It was a clear sign of dismissal, and Amy went away, without having solved her personal dilemma of how she was to work with Max Bentley at least twice a week in close proximity.

Would her resolve not to become further involved with him on anything but a friendly or professional level hold? Could she sustain her cool attitude? Only time would tell. At least she would do her best to maintain only the slenderest thread of contact with him outside the Clinic.

The morning passed quickly enough. Amy escorted elderly or infirm patients to the various doctors and helped them undress, took notes and arranged follow-up appointments, or organised them to see other specialists in the building. It wasn't exactly onerous or testing of her nursing ability, but it was something that had to

be done. It helped in the smooth running of the Clinic
and gave the doctors more time to attend their patients,
which was what St Anne's was all about—medical
excellence.

Amy was on an early lunch, which meant she was
able to dash along to the nearby wine bar and snatch a
sandwich before they got too busy. She even had time
to make a few purchases against her lengthy Christmas
list. Being ill had played havoc with her usually well
organised preparations for the festival, and this year she
had more presents to send away, as most of her friends
were at her old training hospital.

It was as she hurried into the Cathedral bookshop,
directly across the cobbled square from St Anne's, that
Max looked out of his surgery window above the square
and saw her. He stood riveted to the spot, thinking what
a delightful picture she made. Her short, thick, tawny
bright hair, glowed like a shaggy chrysanthemum above
an emerald-green scarf wound round her neck and
streaming down her back over the shabby suede car
coat. Her short skirt revealed several tantalising inches
of silk-covered legs, before they disappeared into calf-
high boots.

She held the door open for a woman with a pram and
a toddler in tow to leave the shop. The two women
exchanged comments, and for a moment Amy's gentle,
animated face was turned towards Max. It seemed to
the watching doctor that all that was best in a young
woman shone out from Amy's face at that moment. He
had, of course, the advantage of knowing something of
her history, and the fact that she was a caring person
both at work and at home. But the way she bent to
touch the toddler's head and peer into the pram quite
transfixed him, and, he was sure, would have told him
much even had she been a stranger.

He made a sudden decision: he would leave the notes from his morning surgery, enter them on the computer later, and take an early lunch break. Amy would be working with him this afternoon, but he had a large clinic and there would be little or no time for personal conversation. If he hurried, he might catch her while she was in the bookshop.

Her coolness with him earlier that morning in the car park bothered him still, though he had put it out of his mind while dealing with patients. Perhaps she hadn't been feeling well? He was not entirely convinced she was ready to start work, in spite of her own conviction that she was, even after yesterday's somewhat traumatic incident.

At least he had a cast-iron excuse to speak to her, since he had eventually succeeded in getting news from the hospital about the injured girl. It was easy to ignore the fact that he could relay this to Amy when she assisted him that afternoon.

He flung his charcoal grey wool topcoat round his shoulders and hurried from his surgery. Impatiently, because the lift didn't arrive the minute he pressed the button, he ran down the gracious staircase with shallow treads, taking them two at a time.

As he stepped out of the elegant front door of St Anne's, a voice hailed him, and there was Belinda. She looked delightful in an outfit of blue and purple. For once everything about her seemed co-ordinated, from the cowl-like pale blue folds of velvet draped round her head to the purple-black high-heeled boots on her feet.

'Max, how wonderful to see you! I was going to call for Amy, but you'll do even better.' She slipped an arm beneath his, and without obviously shaking her off Max could do nothing but allow her arm to remain entwined with his.

He looked with growing frustration towards the book-shop. Amy should still be there. Perhaps he could persuade Belinda to go away for a few minutes, while he tackled her older sister. He gave Belinda one of his scorching smiles.

'I was going for a drink and a bite in the pub,' he lied cheerfully, 'but I have to catch a colleague first.' He waved his arm vaguely across the square. 'Look, you go on to the Cathedral Arms and order something, and I'll join you as soon as I can.'

Belinda pouted. 'Oh, food,' she said crossly. 'Is that all you think about? Look, it won't take long to help me find something really super for someone special.' She pulled at his sleeve with her free hand. 'Oh, come on, Max, don't be a bore! I'd really appreciate your advice—you see, he's quite a bit older than I am, and very distinguished, rather like you, in fact.'

Max made another quick decision. There was no chance of getting rid of Belinda, if she was determined to get her own way. It wouldn't be very satisfactory, meeting up with Amy with her sister in tow, but it would be better than nothing.

'An older man,' he said thoughtfully. 'Do you have any idea what his taste in literature is, or art? I think perhaps a book, or a reproduction print.' He steered her across to the bookshop.

But Belinda stood firmly in front of him when they reached the other side of the square. 'No, nothing as dull as that,' she said scathingly. 'I thought cufflinks, or a really super silk cravat and a tiepin.'

'My dear girl, have you any idea how much any of those things will cost, if they're halfway decent, that is?'

Belinda flushed a delightful pink as she looked up at him and laid a hand on his arm. 'I know they cost the earth, Max, that's why it's so great meeting you to help me choose the right thing. You see, I've had a win on a Premium Bond, enough so that I can really go to town on a present for him. Something he'll appreciate, being older.'

Her eyes shone with happiness and excitement as she pleaded with him. He wasn't sure he liked the way she kept harping on about age; even though her opinion wasn't important to him, nobody liked being constantly reminded that they were not in the first flush of youth!

He gave in and put aside his desire to see Amy. He would make time this afternoon to have a chat with her, even if it wasn't until the end of the clinic.

'Very well,' he said. 'I'm not sure I should be encouraging you, you horrible infant, in your predilection for an older man, but you might as well get the poor chap something he can use, and I believe I shall be a better judge of that than you.'

'Oh, Max, you angel!' smiled a delighted Belinda, and stretched up to kiss him. 'You won't say anything to Amy, will you? I was going to pretend to her that I was getting a present for Trevor from my set, and we were all clubbing together.'

Max stared down at her and put his hands on her shoulders. 'Now look here, Belinda,' he said, grim-voiced. 'Helping you choose a present for a possibly unsuitable man is one thing, deceiving Amy is quite another. Come on, we're going to talk about this.'

It was at that moment that Amy, having made some purchases, put her hand on the door-handle as she prepared to leave the shop. Between the labels advertising various charge cards, and titles of new books, she saw Belinda's kiss and the way Max bent and placed loving hands on her shoulders, before he took her arm and they walked from the square together.

If she had any doubts about his feelings for Belinda,

and hers for Max, the kiss, the way he had touched her, and the proprietorial fashion with which he led her from the square, would have convinced her of the reality. Swallowing her hurt and her tears, Amy hurried back to St Anne's.

Several times during the busy clinic that afternoon Max tried to introduce a personal quality into their conversation, but without success. Amy wasn't even icily cool, a condition in women that he had met before, and could have dealt with by exerting charm and genuine understanding. She was simply professional and cheerfully friendly, but unbreachable.

She came nearest to showing emotion when he reported the latest news of the young woman injured in the accident.

'Terry Foulds,' he told Amy, as she busied herself at the small steriliser on a side table in his surgery, 'the orthopaedic consultant at the General, thinks they might have to do a below-knee amputation, but he's going to try to repair the fragmented bones first, though it will be a long, painful process, and not necessarily successful.'

'I'm sure the patient would be prepared to suffer to save her leg,' commented Amy.

'Yes—apparently as soon as she regained consciousness she said that she'd go through anything rather than have an amputation.'

'Well, that doesn't surprise me,' Amy remarked, sounding almost curt. 'Does it surprise you?'

She was suddenly overwhelmed by his presence, by the memory of the fear in his voice when he had arrived at the scene of the accident the day before. She recalled how he had folded her in his arms as she stumbled to meet him, wet and frightened in the pouring rain.

So, he had been concerned. Well, anyone would be. But it didn't explain the caressing tone he had used as he said her name in the car park this morning, or the way he had held her arm and asked if she was all right. Yet all this tenderness was swamped by the fact that a few hours later he had been with Belinda outside the bookshop, looked down at her with a lover's look, and had protectively taken her arm as they left the square.

The duplicity of the man! How could he pretend such loving concern for her when he was in love with her sister? It wasn't that, though, that troubled her, it was the way he demonstrated his concern that was worrying. After all, he might genuinely exhibit anxiety about his future sister-in-law, but surely he didn't have to do it with such a glint in his eye, such warmth in his voice, as if she, Amy, were all that mattered?

In her misery and distress, because she wanted him to be perfect, and hated him for being two-faced, she momentarily dropped her façade of cheerfulness and pretended to be icily uninterested.

Max stared at her, surprised by the harsh tone in her voice. Why had she suddenly become so hard and cold? She was in fact totally unlike the gentle Amy who had not so long ago bent over the baby in the pram, or who cared for her two younger sisters with such devotion.

He said softly, 'No of course it doesn't surprise me.' For once he could think of nothing more to say, and took refuge in work and brisk efficiency. 'Right, Nurse Kincaid, let's have the next patient in, please.' He glanced at the notes on his desk. 'Mr Bristow, chronic bronchiectasis.'

'Yes, Doctor.' Amy closed the steriliser and moved quietly to the door and ushered in Mr Bristow, with his painful cough and sallow, dehydrated skin.

Somehow she survived the rest of the afternoon and

the penetrating looks that Max gave her from time to time, with his bright, intelligent grey eyes.

She was kept busy enough filling in X-ray and other test forms, giving injections, weighing patients and explaining diet sheets and medication, but it was a relief when the clinic eventually came to an end.

It was a further relief to find Max on the phone when she passed back through the surgery from the tiny clinic-room, where she had been tidying away instruments and dressing packs.

He put his hand over the mouthpiece as she appeared. 'Amy, please wait for a moment,' he pleaded with a smile.

'Sorry, I have an appointment—goodnight.' She hurried from the room, not giving him a chance to say more. Outside in the wide, softly carpeted corridor, now empty of patients, she leaned against the door and breathed a sigh of relief.

It was hell being with him, their hands occasionally touching when he examined a patient and she assisted. Well, she couldn't, without drawing unwelcome attention to the fact, refuse to work with him, but she could keep her distance at home.

Of course, Jenny and the Bentley children were great friends, so she couldn't break off contact with him altogether. And inevitably, as time went on and the relationship between Max and Belinda blossomed, she would have to steel herself to socialise with him in a casual, sisterly fashion. She nearly choked on the word 'sisterly', and swore savagely to herself in the confines of her car as she drove out of Castleminster towards home.

CHAPTER EIGHT

AMY's plan to keep at a distance from Max on home ground was thwarted. The Campions, who for so long had owned and managed the prep school in the village, exercised a great deal of local power and influence. One of their unwritten rules, which all parents seemed only to ready to obey, was that family support was given to pupils at all times, but especially at Christmas, when plays, carol services in school and church, and fund-raising fêtes were almost daily on the agenda.

This clever and manipulative organising of time and talents by the Campions resulted in Amy and Max meeting in the small but well designed hall of the school that very evening.

For some reason, neither had expected to see the other at the school, although knowing the Campions' reputation for raising help, they should have been prepared to meet.

For his part, Max was delighted with the chance to re-establish communication with Amy, happy to dismiss the tension, whatever the cause, that had come between them earlier that day. Over the period of her illness and the short time that he had known her, she had intrigued him with her intelligence and beauty, the latter less obvious than Belinda's but infinitely more lasting, he thought. Native caution, the painful memory of his disastrous marriage, and Amy's own reticence, had prevented him from revealing something of his feelings.

Today, but for the untimely arrival of Belinda, he would have acted on impulse and made an effort to establish some kind of intimate rapport with Amy, away from their families and commitments. He hadn't planned what he was going to say or do when he hoped to meet her in the bookshop, but he had always been good at improvisation and on-the-spot decisions, and usually they paid off. He would have found a way to reach through Amy's reserve and make headway with their relationship.

Now, when Amy appeared in the hall a few minutes after his arrival, he realised he could perhaps salvage the lunchtime fiasco. He went forward to meet her.

'Amy,' he held out both hands in a supplicating gesture, 'please come and rescue me—I'm supposed to be setting up the Crib and draping the figures with cloaks and things. I'm desperate, I need help.'

Amy, whose first reaction when she saw that Max was there was to turn tail and run, found herself smiling in response to his request for help, even as she doubted that it was genuine. If ever there was a man capable of handling a few bits of cloth and drapery, it was Max, with his clever sensitive hands.

'I must see Mrs Campion first and find out what she wants me to do,' she said, trying to sound severe and failing.

Mrs Campion appeared at that moment.

'Amy!' She made a theatrical gesture of surprise. 'You've come, in spite of being ill and caught up in that dreadful accident yesterday!' She pushed several strands of blonded grey hair beneath the felt hat that she habitually wore. 'Now, my dear, we don't want to tax you beyond your strength I wonder. . .' She looked vaguely round the room.

Max said plaintively, 'I could do with some help, setting up the Crib scene for the photograph, and,' he added cunningly, 'I could keep an eye on Amy, see that she doesn't do too much.'

'What a wonderful idea! You help Max, my dear, to get it just right. The photograph is to go on to the front of the programme.' Mrs Campion started to move away, but came back to remind them that the Crib must be dismantled after the photography session, and everything put back in store. 'We set up the Crib again during Advent, in the entrance hall,' she explained.

Amy, who apart from nodding agreement to the arrangement hadn't responded to the deceptively vague Mrs Campion, gazed after the retreating figure of the headmistress-cum-proprietress with a mixture of irritation and admiration.

'She doesn't miss a trick. How does she do it?' She looked round the hall busy with compliant parents hanging curtains and hammering away at various bits of scenery to be used in the children's performance. 'But I don't understand why they use the small crib and figures to photograph, especially as it has to be dismantled afterwards. Why don't they take a picture of the children in rehearsal?'

'Yes, I was puzzled about that, but apparently it's to prevent problems should any of the children playing the major roles back out, get sick, or be blacklisted. It happened on one occasion and caused tears and tantrums when both Mary and the Archangel Gabriel were prevented from appearing, after being photographed on the front of the programme.' Max grinned broadly. 'The mind boggles at what naughtiness they must have committed which prevented them taking part!'

He bent towards Amy and unwound the emerald-green scarf—the one, he noted, that she had been wearing when he had spied her from his surgery window. He said softly, 'I didn't expect to see you tonight, but I'm so glad you're here.'

She ignored his words and the way he had neatly removed her scarf. 'Perhaps they weren't naughty, just off sick or something,' she said, trying to sound severe again and not tremble at his touch.

'Ah, who knows? It was many years ago, and the Campions aren't talking. Suffice to say that the ritual of setting up the small crib to photograph is now as established as Christmas itself.'

Max's whimsical good humour was impossible to resist. Amy began to relax and enjoy herself.

The Crib was not in fact a very small one. The figures of Mary and Joseph and the Christ Child were nearly half life-size. The timbered stable had been erected by Giles Forrester and Theo Grant, two other 'volunteer' parents, and they were now in the process of spreading straw and placing the traditional animals around the stable.

'We've been instructed to dress the chief figures in these,' said Max, undoing the lid of a large old-fashioned truck packed with the predictable robes, cloaks and head dresses deemed appropriate to the Holy Family and the Three Kings. 'The hoi-polloi, of course, in the shape of the shepherds, have to make do with these.' He opened a cardboard carton full of cotton tunics of drab browns and fawns. His eyes gleamed with a kind of sad humour. 'The world hasn't changed much, has it?' he asked.

Giles and Theo went away to fetch more straw, and for a moment, Amy and Max had the vestibule to themselves. They were kneeling on either side of the trunk, which was spilling over with the rich gold and silver robes of the Kings. Max was holding a cloak of gleaming red satin in his hands. He leaned across the trunk and stroked Amy's cheek with the soft material.

'All those poor starving babies,' he murmured softly, 'and ours have got all this!' He indicated the crib and the room in general. His voice was thick with sadness, his grey eyes soft with compassion.

Amy felt her own eyes fill with tears, for the babies and for this man kneeling opposite her, with his reputation for being cold and austere concealing a gentle and loving heart.

'Oh, Max, don't!' She took the rippling crimson robe from him and leaned over to kiss his cheek.

It seemed the most natural thing in the world that he should put his arms round her and help her to her feet, fold her tenderly to him, and lower his lips to hers.

'Oh, Amy, my dearest. . .' His arms dropped and he moved away from her as Giles and Theo made a noisy return, one with his arms full of straw, the other carrying a tray of mulled wine and hot mince pies.

'It's goodies time,' said Giles with a laugh. 'We've all been good children and done our bit, and we're now reaping our reward.'

Somehow Max and Amy got through the rest of the evening, managing to eat, drink and sing appropriate Christmas songs and carols as they and Giles and Theo were joined by other parents who came to see how the Crib was faring.

It was as well that both Max and Amy were used to putting their own problems behind them in order to concentrate on matters in hand. With an effort, they now contrived to do what was expected of them, and clothe the Crib figures as custom demanded, adding, as was also expected, small initiatives and devices of their own.

Even Amy, wrung out by emotion over the thwarted

episode with Max, had to admit that he and she had
acquitted themselves well. The finished assembled figures of the Holy Family and the Three Kings was a
masterpiece of carefully arranged colour and muted
magnificence. The parents, who together with the
Campions gathered in the small foyer to witness the
photographing of the finished piece, made satisfying
exclamations of praise and surprise.

Willing hands helped them to dismantle the Crib and
figures, and both Amy and Max agreed, under a kind of
excited mass hypnosis, to re-erect the Crib as arranged
during Advent.

Since the villagers, and most of the people working in
the school that night, came from within a small radius
of the Green, Amy found herself one of several in the
group disbanding in front of the Doll's House.

'Please come in and have coffee,' she offered, and half
a dozen of her co-workers, including Max, accepted.

Jenny was of course in bed, but Belinda, looking
radiant in a blue velvet housecoat that swept the floor,
let them in and happily busied herself in the kitchen,
dispensing drinks and biscuits with enthusiasm.

Helplessly Amy found herself watching Max, wondering if he would give himself away to Belinda. Would he,
she wondered, follow her sister into the kitchen and kiss
her? Would he by word or gesture convey his love to
Belinda so soon after he had almost kissed her elder
sister?

He remained where he was, sitting in the chair that
had become his during the period that Amy was ill.
Every time she looked towards him, Amy caught his
eye. He didn't look like a man concerned for his
reputation, nor did he seem bothered by Belinda's
presence. Not for the first time, she reached the conclusion that she was unsophisticated where love and

relationships were concerned. Belinda might be younger in years, but she was infinitely older in her understanding of men and attracting the opposite sex.

Max, of course, and others of his kind, understood these things. Presumably he knew that Belinda, young though she was, appreciated the difference between flirting outrageously and a deeper relationship.

But how could he, she thought in anguish when at last everyone left to go home, how could he leave without a special goodbye to her sister? She looked at Belinda, rather expecting to see her showing some signs of distress at Max's seeming indifference, but there was nothing in her sister's demeanour to indicate unhappiness. As soon as everyone had gone, she bade Amy a cheerful goodnight and went upstairs to bed.

Amy decided, herself getting ready for bed a little later, that she must be hopelessly old-fashioned. Perhaps modern girls in love don't expect kisses and endearments, she concluded, and thought it rather sad.

It was a long time before she fell asleep, and her last thoughts were of Max, leaning across the truck in front of the stable and being near to tears on account of the starving babies in the world.

'I do hope Belinda will understand him,' she whispered softly into the darkness, before willing herself to sleep.

CHAPTER NINE

AMY woke the next morning absolutely determined to come to terms with the situation between herself, Belinda and Max. The eternal triangle, she thought, making a face at herself in the mirror, except that the other two don't even know there's a third point.

She couldn't bear to think badly of Max, but the fact remained that he had almost kissed her over the Crib and had only been prevented by the arrival of Giles and Theo. How did that tally with his being in love with Belinda? What an enigma of a man he was! A wonderful doctor, kindness itself when she was ill, and one would have thought a man of integrity. He didn't, couldn't know he was causing her distress, but he must know he was being unfaithful to her sister.

How on earth did he square that with his conscience? That he should do anything underhand simply didn't fit with all the other things she knew about him. He certainly wasn't promiscuous or even given to innocent flirting at work, as some of the other men were. In fact, he had this reputation for being cold and reserved. None of it made sense.

The phone rang. It was a call from the Clinic. Could Amy get in as early as possible? It looked as if there might be a mini flu epidemic brewing, and possibly an outbreak of chickenpox amongst the children.

'There've been several night calls and a good many already this morning,' explained the receptionist who phoned, 'which makes it seem likely. Both Dr Bentley and Dr Love were called two or three times during the night and feel we should be prepared.'

'OK, I'll be in as soon as possible.' Amy put the phone down and set about getting breakfast. Poor Max, she thought, he had to go out after being busy all the evening putting up the Crib, and then. . . Her mind refused to work beyond the point where he had almost kissed her in his distress over the starving babies. She had done all the thinking she could that morning; now she must concentrate on work.

Belinda had already left for college, having taken an early bus into town. At least, thought Amy, her affair with Max has done some good. I don't have to badger her to get up in the mornings, and it can only be his influence making her behave more responsibly.

Once at St Anne's, where every waiting-room seemed full of people, many of whom had come without appointments, she worked flat-out. She and the other nurses, after sorting out the normal clinic chores, shared the job of dealing with patients who appeared to be suffering with flu-like symptoms.

By taking recent histories, temperatures and pulses, they were able to speed the patients to and from the various consulting-rooms. Generally the sifting-out system worked, and patients came out from seeing doctors, with prescriptions for various tablets and elixirs for treating their condition, in record time. It was proof, if proof were needed, that with the whole clinic working as a team, the pressures that an abnormally high number of patients might cause could be relieved. Nobody had to wait too long, and everyone was given proper medical attention.

At the end of the morning, old Dr Rush, the senior GP, visited the staff-room and congratulated those there on the success of the operation.

'Our own little Dunkirk,' he said with heavy humour, and then, looking round at the mostly twenty- to forty-year-old doctors and nurses, added, 'Of course, none of you was around then, but it was backs-to-the-wall time, I can assure you, with more to come. We coped then and we'll cope now, but things might get pretty sticky, so stay alert.'

'Wasn't there a film called *Dunkirk* or something?' asked one very young receptionist.

Dr Rush patted her shoulder as he left the room, and shook his head. 'I don't suppose even your parents were born,' he said, 'when we experienced our obviously misnomered "finest hour". So much for history!'

'No, Doctor, I don't suppose they were,' agreed Samantha, puzzled, but polite.

In the afternoon Amy was sent to Beaminster House, a local retirement home, to give anti-flu injections to the residents.

'A bit like bolting the door after the horse has gone,' said Gerry Love, one of the newer and younger GPs in practice. 'But supplies have been held up until now, and who knows, we might ward off one or two cases.'

He was going to the home too, and offered Amy a lift. 'I've several patients to see,' he explained, 'and will be there for some time. If I've finished before you have, I'll do one or two other nearby visits and collect you afterwards. Do say yes!' he pleaded, his round boyish face, topped with reddish hair, eager and innocent.

He had joined the staff at St Anne's while Amy was off sick, so she knew little about him except that he was generally liked. Ten minutes in his company as they drove to the rest home on the outskirts of the town explained why. He was cheerful and uncomplicated, and didn't hanker after the more glamorous world of hospital in surgery or medicine.

'My dad's in general practice,' he told Amy. 'And even my grandfather still does the odd locum, and he's well in his seventies. I never wanted to be anything else other than a GP, which is just as well, as I wasn't startlingly brilliant in med school.'

'It isn't just being brilliant, though, is it,' said Amy, finding herself drawn to this happy, open young man, 'making the grade in hospital? A lot of it is politics and being in the right place at the right time, knowing the right people, and being prepared to be utterly ruthless if necessary.'

She turned her head and looked out of the side window, for a moment swamped by an unaccustomed wave of bitterness and self-pity as she recalled the futility of falling in love with ambitious medical men on the hospital ladder.

She didn't see Gerry's look of concern.

'Are you all right?' he asked.

'Of course.' She blew her nose hard.

They turned into the tree-lined drive leading to Beaminster House, and Gerry pulled off on to the grass verge amongst the dying and dead blossoms of giant hydrangea bushes. He undid his seatbelt and slewed round in his seat to look at her.

'Here,' he said, 'use this—it's better than that old paper tissue.' He handed her a large white cotton handkerchief. 'I only keep it to lend to damsels in distress to dry their eyes with,' he added with a laugh.

Amy turned and faced him. Just hearing his cheerful silly words made her smile. All at once she felt that life was not quite such a burden; there were other men around besides the sophisticated Max Bentley or those social and professional climbers she had suddenly recalled from the past.

'Oh, Gerry——' she gave him a watery smile '—you are nice! But you shouldn't put yourself down for wanting to be a GP. I think practice doctors are the most important people in medicine. Who else sees such a variety of conditions, who else has to make the decision to further investigate someone with strange symptoms? It's the so-called humble GP who keeps the others in work, after all. They seem to forget that.'

Gerry beamed at her. 'Well, I thought I was going to have to lend you a shoulder to cry on, but, like the marvellous nurse you are, you're hell bent on inflating my ego.'

'But it's true,' she insisted. 'I have very strong views on the subject.'

'And on many others, I bet.'

'Well, yes, I suppose I have.' Amy smiled at him, and he beamed back at her.

'I like that—a strong-minded and attractive woman. Well, I'm footloose and fancy free, as I'm sure old Dr Rush would have said in the dim past. Will you come out for a meal with me one evening when we've got over the worst of this epidemic? I don't think I dare fix anything before then.'

'If you are footloose and whatever, I should love to,' Amy smiled.

She felt a ripple of pleasure at the prospect of spending an evening with Gerry. Here was a man as dedicated to medicine as she was to nursing, yet young and vibrant and without commitments, except to his work. It was suddenly important that she should be free to be herself for once, not a substitute mother to Jenny and Belinda, however much she loved them. Not a sensible career woman with domestic responsibilities, unwisely attracted to her sister's lover, but a reasonably attractive female out to enjoy herself.

'Great, we'll fix it as soon as possible.' Gerry switched on the engine and fastened his seatbelt. 'You're not heavily attached to anyone, are you?' he asked as he drove off the verge and back on to the drive. 'I wouldn't want to encroach.'

'No,' said Amy firmly, 'no attachments.' For good measure she added, 'And I don't want any—not yet, anyway.'

'Fine. No strings, I promise.'

He gave her one of his beaming smiles and took a hand from the wheel to pat her arm. Amy smiled back.

A car came round the bend in the drive at that moment and the driver raised a hand as they slowed to let him pass.

Amy waved in return. 'Dr Grey,' she explained. 'He's my GP and a very nice man, but he doesn't work at St Anne's, so you probably haven't met him.'

'Elliot Grey, I've heard of him. I dare say we'll meet up some time.'

They drew up at the front door of the home, and for the rest of the afternoon Amy was kept busy giving flu jabs, and reassuring the elderly patients.

Max was the first person at the Clinic whom Amy and Gerry met when they returned from Beaminster House. He arrived in the car park as they were getting out of Gerry's car. Amy felt there was something strange about him, that he was even more aloof than usual. He seemed surprised, almost shocked to see them.

Gerry gave him a friendly wave.

'We've just come back from Beaminster House,' he called cheerfully across the park. 'Amy's been giving flu jabs, for what they're worth.'

Max joined them as they walked towards the rear door of the Clinic. Amy was very conscious of his tall, elegant presence. She wondered if he might allude to last night, or make an excuse to speak with her alone.

He did neither.

'Yes, so I understand.' His voice was deep, expression-less. 'I met Elliot Grey at the hospital, and he told me he'd seen you there.'

Amy kept silent, but dared to look surreptitiously at Max, only to find him looking down at her with his flint-grey eyes devoid, as his voice had been, of expression. The freezing cold they conveyed made her shiver, and in the most natural fashion Gerry put his arm around her shoulders.

'A bitter north-easter,' he said. 'Let's hope there's some tea or coffee on the go.' He rang the bell and the door was opened almost at once, and the three of them trooped in to the welcoming warmth of St Anne's.

Amy realised her plans to avoid Max as much as possible when off duty would have to be amended. She must come to terms with seeing a great deal of him in the weeks leading up to Christmas. The village was buzzing with pre-Christmas activity and, in spite of the natives having something of a reputation for being cautious with newcomers, both the Kincaids and the Bentleys were made welcome and found that they were going to be fully involved with all that was going on.

It wasn't surprising that Max and his family were absorbed into Monkton. The Carters, who worked for him, had both been born there, and the Bentleys themselves had past associations with the village. But the Kincaids had no such local connections, and the welcome they were given was inspired entirely by their own efforts to be friendly. Everyone seemed only too

willing to receive the three pretty sisters into their homes
and hearts.

It followed that both families were invited to take
part in various functions, quite apart from those involving the school. Max, Amy and Belinda found themselves
co-opted into the church choir, enlarged over the
Christmas period, to go out on carol-singing sprees to
raise money for various charities.

The local Women's Institute, this year raising funds
for the Castleminster Hospice, asked Amy and Belinda
to manage a stall at the Elizabethan Fair being held in
the village hall. Max was asked to open the Fair as the
local medical celebrity.

On the agenda was a mince pie and mead party, to
be held by the Mothers' Union, a sausage roll and
mulled wine buffet, courtesy of the Rector and 'Mrs
Rector', and a cheese and cider evening, arranged by
the Young Farmers' Club. The crowning glory of all the
fund-raising was the champagne and smoked salmon
evening to be hosted by Sir Daniel and Lady
Charlesworth at Dellicourt House, a magnificent
example of a sixteenth-century manor house lying just
outside the village.

To all these functions Max and Amy and Belinda
were invited. In addition there were daytime events
involving the children. Life looked like being hectic and
astonishingly warm and happy in this season of good
cheer. In spite of her concern over Max's behaviour,
Amy felt that seeing him and Belinda together might be
a little less painful with the promise of friendship with
Gerry Love.

Not, she had to admit, that her sister or the doctor
had ever exhibited many loverlike actions. They seemed
to laugh a lot together, and Max teased Belinda about
everything, from her youthful exuberance to her rather

bizarre manner of dress. Amy wasn't surprised that
Max did not appear overtly demonstrative. He was a
very private man, and not given to showing his feelings
in public, but Belinda was a different matter. She
normally had no inhibitions about revealing her
emotions, so it was rather surprising that she too was
undemonstrative.

Yet for the last week or so she had been happy and
bubbling over with goodwill. Her moodiness had gone
and she seemed to be looking forward to joining in the
village festivities. Amy reasoned that this was because
she had Max's devotion and undying love, and was
prepared to wait for him to declare it openly. That he
didn't, Amy thought, was perhaps because he was a
little ashamed of having shown untimely and unaccept-
able feelings towards herself. She couldn't think of any
other reason for his holding back with Belinda.

He had always been polite and courteous where she
was concerned, but after the near-kiss of the 'Crib
night', as she thought of it, he made no attempt to be
alone or intimate with her. She had a peculiar feeling
that his restraint was in some way connected with her
visit to Beaminster House and the meeting in the car
park. Though why she felt like this eluded her.

She was grateful, though, for his coolness, for she had
no idea how she would have coped had he become
amorous. His strong and masculine charm overwhelmed
her whenever she was near him. She was ashamed, for
Belinda's sake, of what had happened at Campion's
when they were erecting the Crib, and concluded that
Max was too, which was why he was now keeping his
distance.

She couldn't pretend that his aloofness didn't hurt,
but at least she did not now have to consider him a two-
faced monster. He might not yet have officially claimed

Belinda, but he was not playing a two-handed game involving both sisters. His integrity, as far as she was concerned, might be dented by his actions on that one occasion, but it was not irreparably smashed, since he wasn't pursuing her any more, but concentrating on Belinda.

The flu epidemic continued to escalate, but failed to reach the proportions that were at first feared, although new cases were added to the list daily, and everyone was kept busy. The organising of the medical and nursing facilities at the clinic continued to pay dividends. The extra work that the flu and the minor outbreak of chickenpox produced was handled with the minimum of disruption to the regular programme.

Max was one of the doctors most affected by the flu bug, since a number of patients developed chest conditions arising out of the infection. Inevitably too, some of his regular patients picked up the bug, which aggravated their chronic state. His clinics became busier as the other practitioners sent patients to him for specialist evaluation and treatment.

As his regular clinic nurse, Amy was naturally involved in the extra workload.

In the middle of the clinic a few days later, following her visit to Beaminster House, Max asked, 'Would you be prepared to do some extra hours for the next few weeks, Amy? I realise that with Christmas looming and all the goings on in the village life's going to be hectic, but I could do with more help and extended clinics.'

As always, the way he said her name made it sound something special. She carefully finished disposing of the syringe and needle used for the last patient into the specific receptacles, before turning to face him.

'Yes, of course, so long as it's necessary.'

'My dear girl, I wouldn't ask if it were not. You have
enough on your plate without adding more burdens.'
His grey eyes looked directly into hers and held her for
a moment spellbound. She took in a deep breath, and
with an effort turned away from him. He reached out
and caught her by the wrist as she was about to pass.
'Amy,' his voice was husky, charged with emotion, 'I'm
sorry about the other night when we were setting up the
Crib. I thought I'd read the signs correctly, but
obviously I hadn't. But please don't hold it against me.'

Amy stared at him in astonishment. What was he
saying—what did he mean? Because of his recent and
welcome reticence, she was astounded by his sudden
gesture and the warmth of his voice. She groped for
words.

'Max, I don't know what you mean. What has that
got to do with anything? That was personal and should
never have happened; this is nursing business—I don't
see any connection.'

He continued to hold her wrist.

'No, you're quite right, this isn't the time or place,
but what with the village activities and the social round
in which we'll be involved, I wanted to explain while I
have the chance. I'm sorry if I embarrassed you the
other evening, but it won't happen again. You need to
get out and enjoy yourself, you have more than your fair
share of responsibility. It's only natural that you should
want younger company.'

Amy stared at him. He was talking rubbish, yet he
looked his usual calm, distinguished self. Only his voice,
deeper than usual with emotion, gave him away. If, as
he seemed to be saying, she might find him too mature
with too many commitments to make him attractive to
her, then what made him think the even younger
Belinda found him acceptable? And he spoke as if

Belinda wasn't important, as if what he was saying had nothing to do with her. It didn't make sense.

She wished he would let go of her wrist; his touch, as always, was making her feel most peculiar. Perhaps it was because they were in his consulting-room, with patients waiting just outside to see him, that his long, cool fingers on her warm flesh assumed an even greater degree of intimacy.

The telephone rang. For a moment his restraining hand continued to encircle her wrist, then with a half groan, half sigh, he relinquished it and picked up the receiver.

'Dr Bentley,' he said briskly into the mouthpiece. 'Yes, of course I'll see him—right. Mr Steel, flu, possible inflammation of lungs, very congested, recent stroke, somewhat confused. Right, Gerry, I'll ask Amy to fetch him, I'm sure she'll be only too pleased to do that.'

'Another patient to add to the list?' Amy asked gently, all anger washed from her voice as she looked at the tired doctor sitting at his desk.

It's not fair, she thought, he's being pressed too hard, getting more than his share of work. His earlier words and actions, heavy with emotion, and on a personal level, were still extraordinary, but any sense of being manipulated by him fled in the face of his slumped shoulders and the general air of sadness that now engulfed him.

''Fraid so—an elderly chap who picked up this bug last week. Because he's had a recent stroke, he's more than usually congested. He's a patient of Gerry Love—he'll give you all the gen when you collect Mr Steel's records from him.' He raised a smile and his well marked eyebrows. His grey eyes glinted. 'Go on, Nurse, get going, and don't rush back, I can cope with the next couple of patients unaided. You go and have a chat with Gerry.'

It was as if he wanted her to spend time with Gerry Love, Amy thought, as she made her way to the lift and the second floor where Gerry and his partners had their offices. But why, why had he made all those peculiar and unrelated remarks about friendship and age? What did it all mean?

Gerry was waiting for her in the doorway of his consulting-room. She had no difficulty in identifying Mr Steel, who was sitting in the waiting area, an obvious stroke victim, with his head on one side, a walking frame, and a useless leg stuck out in front of him.

'Come in,' said Gerry, with his usual wide smile. 'Nice of Max to send you in person.'

Amy frowned. 'Well, I am his clinic nurse, it seems only natural that I should come for Mr Steel and his notes.'

'Yes, well, perhaps. I offered to get the reception nurse to escort him, but he seemed hell-bent on sending you. Perhaps he's intent on furthering our. . . friendship?'

'Don't you start talking in riddles!' she exclaimed, half angry, half amused. 'I've had enough of that for one day, thank you very much!'

'Riddles?' he queried.

'Oh, forget it. Look, give me Mr Steel's notes and I'll be on my way.'

'Hey, don't take it out on me, whatever it is! I just made a normal inter-house call for specialist opinion. It was your boss who brought in a personal element.'

Amy felt sorry for Gerry. He was patently sincere and surprised by her prickly reaction. Well, she reasoned, why shouldn't he be? He hadn't been subjected to the incoherent ramblings of one of the senior physicians practising in St Anne's. A physician who had already made a name for himself as aloof, reserved and autocratic, though admired by the medical and more senior of the nursing staff. But a man whom she knew to be emotionally vulnerable, as capable of giving way to impulse as any of the lesser men who worked at the clinic.

Why over the last few days had Max seemed almost to avoid her? What had happened to change his attitude, and had it changed his attitude towards Belinda? Why hadn't her sister, if for some reason Max was reluctant, said something about their love and intentions?

Life, which in the autumn seemed set on a comfortable course, through November, her illness, the accident, and Max's relationship with both herself and Belinda, had become complicated. Well, tomorrow would be the first of December, a new month. The village events would kick off with the Elizabethan Fair. Amy, ever optimistic, looked forward to the last month of the year with hope.

She took the notes from Gerry's hands.

'Thanks,' she said, flashing him a smile. 'Take no notice of me, I've had a hell of an afternoon.'

He looked relieved. 'We might be able to fix up a date,' he said, 'now that the bug is under control.'

'What about starting off by coming to our Elizabethan Fair tomorrow, and spending a lot of money on our stall?' suggested Amy.

'Our stall?' he queried.

'My sister and I are in charge of the books and pictures. You could come back to tea afterwards at the Doll's House.'

He looked astonished. 'The Doll's House?' he echoed.

'It's the name of our cottage on the village green,' explained Amy. 'It's very small.'

Gerry beamed. 'It sounds delightful, like something out of the Brothers Grimm or Hans Andersen. Very romantic!'

'Well, it's home,' said Amy in a matter-of-fact voice, 'and you'd be very welcome.'

'I'd love to come, work permitting.'

'Right, see you tomorrow, then.'

'Yes, see you.'

Gerry went out into the waiting-room with her and introduced her to Mr Steel.

'Nurse Kincaid will take you to see Dr Bentley,' he told the elderly man. 'He'll be able to do something about that rattly old chest of yours.' He was very kind.

The patient grimaced, trying to smile. He dribbled as he attempted to answer. Gerry looked at him with compassion, and Amy thought how lucky she was to be working with such understanding and humanitarian doctors.

'Come on, Mr Steel,' she helped him stand up, 'let's tootle along to the lift.' She smiled at the old man as she set his walking frame in position.

He grasped the steel frame, and tried to say something.

'Say it again, Mr Steel,' said Amy, leaning over so that she could watch his mouth movements.

'S. . . Sh. . . Shteel,' he mumbled through his slack, uncontrollable lips. He banged the walking frame hard with his good hand. 'Shteel,' he pointed at himself.

Suddenly Amy understood. She laughed, and Mr Steel grimaced happily. 'Steel,' she said, patting what was probably the aluminium frame of his walker, 'and so are you.'

'Yes,' for a moment his voice was quite clear, 'Steel.' He put a hand on his chest, and, though he wheezed alarmingly, Amy realised he was telling her that he was tough.

They moved into the lift and rode down to the first floor, where Max was waiting.

CHAPTER TEN

THE following day dawned bright and frosty. It was the first of December, and the day of the Elizabethan Fair. Amy looked out of her tiny window overlooking the Green. It looked as smooth as an iced cake in the early morning sunshine. Her determination to make the most the new month and the Christmas preparations, and her growing friendship with Gerry Love, was still with her.

Life was full of delicious possibilities.

Jenny bounced into her room, as usual smiling and happy.

She gave Amy a hug. 'Isn't it a lovely morning?' she said. 'All Christmassy with the frost. I wonder if it will snow for Christmas.' She added wistfully, 'Do you remember how it snowed at the beginning of November, when you were ill and Dr Max came in every day and I stayed with Rose and Harry?'

'Yes, I remember,' said Amy softly, kneeling at the low windowsill with one arm about Jenny's waist.

'Wasn't it a happy time, Amy, once you weren't too ill?'

'Yes, love, it was.'

'I wish Dr Max came every day now; he hasn't been in for ages,' sighed Jenny.

'He came the other night after we'd been helping at the school, but you were in bed, of course,' Amy added.

'Oh, I know that,' Jenny's pretty round face was screwed up in a frown. 'But it's not the same somehow, it's not like when he was our special friend, and used to just come in and out, and bring logs for the fire.'

Amy caught her breath. It was true, although Jenny was only talking about a couple of weeks or so, which to her seemed a long time; it was strange that Max didn't come more often to see Belinda. Of course, they'd been frantically busy at the clinic, he especially, and that could account for it, but since the day she had seen Max and Belinda outside the bookshop and here that one evening, they had not met, to her knowledge.

Of course, they might have done, in Castleminster perhaps on evenings when Belinda was late back from college. In fact, that was probably why Belinda spent so much time in the town—she was meeting Max. Of course, they would be too much in the public eye in the village. It must be difficult for them to have time together without being with their respective families or under the gaze of the locals.

It hurt to think of them needing privacy, but it made sense, and she was determined to be happy for them and hope they would soon be open about their relationship. In a way, that would make things easier. Amy gave herself a mental shake. She had the Fair to look forward to this afternoon, and Gerry's visit.

She gave Jenny a kiss. 'Come on, love, let's go down and have breakfast and do our lists for our shopping. We're going to have a lovely day.'

Jenny was at once diverted, and tucked into her bacon and egg, a weekend treat, as she chattered happily about what she was going to buy. Belinda had gone in to college on an early bus, for a special Saturday lecture. She was to meet her sisters for an early lunch at White's, the old-fashioned tea parlour near the Cathedral.

'You may have one cup of milky coffee,' Amy told

Jenny, as she ground the beans and the kitchen filled
with a rich aroma. Weekends were special times when
they modified their self-imposed healthy diet of low-fat,
low caffeine and low-alcohol diet to accommodate a few
treats.

'Brilliant!' said Jenny cheerfully. 'May I have a mug,
please, it's bigger?'

Both she and Amy giggled at her obvious deception.

The front doorbell rang, and Amy whipped off her
pretty half-apron, before going to answer it.

Max stood there, leaning against the door-jamb,
smiling, composed, elegant in a casual fashion. He was
wearing a rather ancient, though impeccably cut, tweed
suit over a lemon-coloured crew-necked pullover.

'Hi,' he said, smiling at Amy in a friendly manner.
'Do you think I might come in? I want to put a
proposition to you.'

The sight of him standing on her doorstep caused her
to breathe in sharply, and she was conscious of her
breasts straining against the cashmere of her emerald-
green sweater as she pressed herself against the wall to
let him through.

'Delightful!' he murmured, not even pretending not
to notice as he slid past her. His grey eyes, that could
be cool, or steely, or warmly blue, now glinted with
appreciation as he stared down unabashed at her ample
curves. Somehow he managed to bend and brush her
forehead with his lips. 'So wholesome,' he said softly. 'It
was the first thing I noticed about you Amy, your
wholesomeness, your fragrance.'

'Do go through,' said Amy, trying to sound cool and
unaffected by his presence without sounding rude.
'We're in the kitchen having breakfast. At least, Jenny
and I are. I'm afraid you've missed Belinda, she had to

go into college for a special lecture quite early, even though it is a Saturday.'

Max grinned down at her. 'Well, what a long speech,' he said in a teasing voice, and added, taking the small hall in a few strides, 'and what a delicious smell—ah, freshly ground coffee beans!' He turned to look at her just before entering the kitchen. 'Brazilian?' he asked.

'Yes. Would you like a cup?'

'Might it be a mug? It's bigger.'

They were in the kitchen now, and both the Kincaid sisters burst out laughing. Max looked puzzled.

'Is it that hilarious?' he asked.

Jenny her small face wreathed in smiles, explained. 'I just asked for a mug because it's bigger. Amy only lets me have coffee at weekends as a treat. She says too much caffeine is bad. Do you think it's bad, Dr Max?'

'Certainly, especially for under-twelves.'

'Amy says too much caffeine is bad even for grown-ups.'

Max grinned, and his lean face looked, as always, less lined, younger, when he smiled.

'And who am I to argue with your clever sister?' he asked, his grey eyes gleaming as they locked on to Amy's. She felt herself blushing, and turned hurriedly away. His eyes, beneath their innocent gaze, were too penetrating, too questioning, too knowing.

She bustled over to the coffee percolator and made a production out of pouring him coffee, while Jenny, oblivious of the exchange between them, chatted away.

'You had a proposition to put forward,' Amy said, valiantly trying to make her voice sound casual as she placed a mug of coffee in front of him.

'Yes, if you can manage it, I thought we might all get together after the Fair and the children's rehearsal at school. Have tea at my place. We've all been so busy

lately that we've hardly seen each other socially, and
you and Belinda will be glad of a break after manning a
stall all the afternoon.'

The speech was spoken to her and Jenny, but Amy
was sure it would have been intended for Belinda had
she been there. Perhaps Max hadn't seen much of her
sister; perhaps he wanted to declare himself at last. The
variations on why he had suddenly come up with his
suggestion were endless.

If she hadn't known better, known that he was in love
with Belinda and anxious for her company, she would
have wondered if. . . She shied away from the possibility
that he might be interested in her for herself and not
because she was Belinda's sister. The idea was ridiculous, in spite of his flattering remark in the hall minutes
before. All his kindnesses, all his efforts to ease the
situation when she was ill, with the exception of his
near-kiss over the Crib, had been made because she was
Belinda's sister, surely!

Even his one fall from grace had been triggered off by
his distress over the deprived children of the world.
Surely that was commendable? There had been odd
incidents at the surgery, notably yesterday when he had
spoken in apparent riddles about youth and responsibility. That remained a mystery.

When Amy gathered her wits and brought herself
back to the warm aromatic kitchen in the Doll's House,
it was to hear Jenny excitedly agreeing that the Bentleys
and Kincaids should spend the evening together.

Firmly, but she hoped not repressively, she pointed
out that they were expecting a guest for tea.

'Gerry Love's coming,' she told Max. 'Well, that is if
he can get away. He's on call.'

Both Jenny and Max looked taken aback for a

moment, and Amy heard herself suggesting that the Bentleys joined them here in the cottage for tea.

'Oh, lovely, lovely!' Jenny sang out. 'It'll be just like it used to be, Dr Max, when Amy was ill, and you came in every day. We were just talking about that this morning, Amy, weren't we?'

'Yes,' confirmed Amy, avoiding Max's eye.

'So,' he sipped at his fragrant mug of coffee and twinkled at Amy through the steam from his drink. 'It's on for tonight—the children will be pleased, and I'm delighted.'

Amy, who had sat down at the table to drink her own coffee, looked across at him.

'Yes.' She tried not to sound breathless. 'We'll all come back here for tea.' She gathered up a few plates and added deliberately, 'You and your children, Belinda, *Gerry*, and we two.' She put her hand on Jenny's shoulder and squeezed it. 'It'll be great fun, won't it, Jen?' For once she used Belinda's diminutive easily. 'Having all our friends here.'

'Brilliant,' said Jenny, beaming at her and Max.

'I look forward to it,' said Max evenly, and his eyes caught and held Amy's yet again, but this time with intelligence and understanding, and nothing more evocative. 'I must be on my way.' He stood up, and Amy was conscious of his height and breadth. He seemed to fill the kitchen with his body and his personality. 'Thanks for the coffee, caffeine and all—it was delicious.' He bent forward and kissed Amy on the tip of her nose.

'And me,' said Jenny, and obligingly he bent and kissed her small upturned nose too.

Shopping, pretending an interest in buying presents, lunching at White's, passed by Amy as in a dream. She must have seemed reasonably normal to Jenny, who would have commented otherwise, and who had obviously had a wonderful morning. And Belinda, when she joined them, also seemed unaware of anything strange in Amy.

Amy let her sisters choose what they and she should eat.

'Honestly, I don't mind what I have,' she said. 'You know me—as long as it's not meat, I'll eat anything.'

'Even the most expensive things?' asked Jenny.

'Why not? It's Christmas, let's splash out.'

Christmas, she thought, and Max had kissed the tip of my nose as though he meant it. For once she deliberately subdued her conscience and gave herself up to the sheer pleasure of recalling his kiss. It didn't matter that as they were pushing and weaving their way through hundreds of other shoppers, plain common sense told her it was madness to think of Max Bentley as anything other than her future brother-in-law. Just this time, just for a little while, she wanted to hug the memory of his kiss, and the look that he gave her as he left, to herself.

She wanted to pretend that he meant it, that he was in love with her, as she knew, and had known for some time, that she was in love with him. She ate her lunch in a state of euphoria, but so cleverly disguised her feelings that neither of her sisters even began to suspect what was happening to her.

Astonishingly, it was Belinda, not generally given to keeping good time, who suggested that they should return home and get changed for the Fair.

'Yes, of course,' Amy said happily. 'We mustn't be late for the Fair.' Because, she added to herself, Max will be there, looking handsome and elegant and so self-contained as he gives his opening speech.

Feeling as if she were floating, she followed the other

two from the restaurant and drove the three of them
back to Monkton.

Max's speech was everything that might be expected of
him—witty at times, serious when it needed to be, when
he was speaking of the hospice and the care that the
patients there required. He reminded everyone present
that their money spent on the White Elephant stall, or
having their fortunes told, or buying secondhand goods,
would all go to help in easing the suffering of those at
the Castleminster Hospice.

'Somewhere,' he added as a rider to his main speech,
'where any one of us could end up if we have the
misfortune to fall chronically sick. And if we did, we'd
be glad we were in the Castleminster Hospice, where
tender loving care is an everyday fact, and practised by
all the staff, at all times.'

He received thunderous applause, before his audience
dispersed to spend a hectic few hours buying from the
stalls and purchasing the various draw tickets on offer.
Amy and Belinda's books and bric-à-brac stall did a
roaring trade, not least, although they were not aware
of it, because they looked delightful in their vaguely
Elizabethan costumes, all high ruffled necklines and
tightly corseted waists.

Gerry Love arrived towards the end of the afternoon.

'I'm so sorry I'm late,' he apologised to Amy. 'Had a
couple of emergencies.'

'It doesn't matter,' said Amy gaily, her euphoria still
with her. 'There are still things left to buy, and the
draws haven't been made yet. As soon as Belinda gets
back she can take you round the stalls.'

'I'd rather you took me round the stalls,' said Gerry,
giving her a friendly leer.

'You won't, not when you meet my sister,' Amy laughed. 'She's lovely, and great fun.'

Just then Belinda returned from the cloakroom, and Amy introduced Gerry to her. From the moment they touched hands and spoke, Amy knew that something momentous had happened between them. It was like watching a tableau, or the final scene in one of the great romantic movies.

'Hello,' said Gerry, his voice husky. He cleared his throat.

'Hi,' murmured Belinda, and took in a deep breath. 'Amy's told me so much about you.'

Amy blinked. As far as she knew she had simply announced that Gerry might be coming to tea.

Gerry kept Belinda's hand in his, and it was then that Amy realised Max had lost her. Oh, poor Max, she thought, he'll be devastated—or will he? The second treacherous thought came as she recalled his feather-light kisses, his words and the way he had looked at her that morning.

A wave of happiness engulfed her as she took in what had happened between Belinda and Gerry. Her thoughts raced away like mad. If Belinda had fallen for Gerry, and, astonishing as it seemed, Gerry had fallen for her, neither he nor Belinda would be hurt. Could something so wonderful, so crazy, happen like that? Had it happened here, in the hustle and bustle of the village hall, or was she deluding herself?

No, she wasn't, at least not where Belinda and Gerry were concerned. Their future was sealed with a hand-shake, a smile and a few prosaic words, she was sure of it. About Max she was not so sure, but she could hope— hope and pray. The elation with which she had started the day came back in full force. Life was full of delicious possibilities.

At that moment Max detached himself from the group of worthy ladies who had been escorting him round all the afternoon and made his way over to their stall. He clapped Gerry on the shoulder. 'Glad you could make it,' he said cordially.

Gerry dropped Belinda's hand and went pink.

'Yes, so am I. You know what it's like.'

'Indeed.' Max continued to sound friendly and cheerful. Amy thought she detected an undercurrent of—what?

She looked at each man in turn, but except for Gerry's blush, and he was prone to this, there was nothing to indicate that anything was wrong. Could Max have been aware of the electric situation between the two young people?

It was at that moment that young Richard Dent, a Scout helping at the Fair, passed out, and Max, Gerry and Amy automatically began giving him first aid.

Richard had grazed his head against the side of the stall as he fell to the ground, and this bled spectacularly for a few moments in the way that even superficial head wounds often did. Neither the doctors nor Amy were unduly concerned about this minor problem, but the sight of blood raised a concerted gasp of shocked surprise from the crowd of helpers gathered around the prone body.

'Will you please stand back and give the boy some air,' said Max in a friendly but firm voice. And to Amy. 'Fish out the handkerchief from my top pocket and make a pressure pad to apply to that.' He nodded toward the boy's head. 'You can fix it with my cravat.'

His own hands were busy keeping the boy's head turned to one side and taking his pulse. Amy knelt down beside him and slipped the silk scarf from round his neck.

Even under pressure of the emergency, she was sensitive to being close to him. To touching his neck as she removed the cravat, to noticing the fuzz of grey-black hair where it curled against his shirt collar.

Very slightly her fingers trembled, and Max must have felt their movement, for he looked up from his crouching position and his eyes met hers for the briefest moment.

Amy caught her breath and turned her head away from his intense gaze. She couldn't possibly have seen in his eyes what she thought she saw, could she? She turned back to look at him again, but his head was already lowered over the inert form on the floor.

He murmured something to Gerry, and together they turned the still unconscious boy into a recovery position on his side, with his right arm extended behind him, right leg straight and left leg bent at the knee to tilt him slightly forward. His left arm was crooked in front of him and his chin extended to push his head back and keep airways open.

Max felt his pulse. 'Rapid, shallow,' he reported tersely. He lightly touched Richard's pale cheek, wet with sweat, and lifted his eyelids to check the pupils and assess the depth of unconsciousness. 'He'll be round soon,' he said, a note of relief in his voice. 'Could be a hypoglycaemic collapse.' He bent over the boy again and sniffed at his mouth. 'Nothing, quite odourless—a pretty sure sign of a diabetic coma, wouldn't you say?'

Gerry nodded.

'Sugar?' queried Amy.

Gerry felt in the pockets of Richard's windcheater, and shook his head.

Amy looked up at the circle of faces all staring down at the boy. 'Will somebody please fetch a sweet drink, hot or cold will do, and a spoon?' she said.

Two or three women all moved away towards the refreshment table, obviously relieved to have something to do.

A man's voice said from the back of the crowd, 'Young Rick can't have no sugar, he's got diabetes or something. I don't suppose you knew that, Doc? Sugar'll kill him!'

'Not in this case it won't,' replied Max calmly. 'Nurse Kincaid is quite right to ask for it. It will save this young chap.' He smiled towards the man who had spoken. 'But you were quite right to mention it—it might have been the wrong thing to do. I'd be glad to explain it to you some time.'

'Well, I don't understand it,' muttered the man. 'Young Rick's mother told me that he mustn't have sugar at any price.'

Richard began to come round. He twitched a little, and moaned before opening his eyes. They were very blue, and frightened.

'It's all right, Richard, everything's under control,' Max explained quietly. 'You passed out for a little while—perhaps you forgot your insulin or bypassed your usual diet?'

Richard mumbled something unintelligible, and Amy bent over him. 'Here,' she said. 'Drink this, it will make you feel better.'

Richard sipped from the spoon that she offered him, and after another sip Amy offered him the carton to drink from.

'Gosh, that's better,' he said. His skin was already less clammy, and when Max took his pulse again, he reported that it was a better speed and volume.

'Stay there for a bit,' advised Max. 'I'm going to have a word with your GP on the phone. I think that's Dr Grey, yes?'

'Yes.' The boy shivered, and Belinda, who had been standing immobile up to now, seemed to gather herself together. She produced from behind the stall a long, elegant stole of finest mohair and gently laid it over the boy.

'It's not really your colour,' she said with a laugh, 'but it's warm.'

'Yeah, it's warm all right,' Richard agreed faintly, looking at Belinda admiringly. 'Thanks.'

Belinda blushed, and Amy noticed Gerry looking at her sister, also admiringly.

'It's no big deal,' Belinda murmured.

Amy was pleased with her for being so practical and thoughtful.

Max came back. 'Dr Grey wants me to arrange for you to go into hospital, Richard, just for a check-up—make sure that your maintenance insulin is correct and confirm that your head injury isn't serious.' The boy made a face, and Max added, 'They may not even keep you in overnight, just see you in Casualty and do a blood test.'

'What about my mum, she'll be expecting me home for tea?'

'I'm sure somebody will call and let her know what's happened.' Max looked at the circle of people still standing around.

'I'll go and tell your mum,' said the man who had spoken out about Rick being a diabetic.

'Good,' said Max. 'That's kind of you—I'm sure you'll break it gently. Does your mother drive?' he asked Rick. 'Will she be able to get to the hospital?'

The boy shook his head. 'No, she's not well, Doctor, but Mr Moore can tell her not to worry. I'll get the bus home if they let me out tonight, and my mate Kevin will bring things in to me if I've got to stay there. He'll be calling in home when he gets back from work, so he'll know what's happened.'

Amy thought, he's trying to be brave about this, poor boy, but he must be feeling lonely. 'Look,' she said, 'I'll go and collect my car and follow the ambulance in to the hospital. If you need things to be brought in I can let your friend know, otherwise I can bring you back.'

'No need for that,' said Max. 'I'm taking him in my car. Quicker than waiting for the ambulance,' he added casually. He gave Amy a smile that made her catch her breath. 'But I'd be grateful for your company and as escort for Richard, if you can manage it.' He looked from her to Gerry Love, as if asking his colleague if that was all right with him.

Amy said quickly, 'I'm sure Gerry won't mind if I go, even though he's my visitor. Belinda will look after him and give him tea. You don't mind, do you Gerry?' she asked, knowing that nothing would suit him better. Whatever his intention had been about cementing his friendship with her when he'd accepted her invitation had been submerged when he met Belinda.

Gerry, blushing to the roots of his fair, reddish hair, shook his head. 'Of course I don't mind, it's all in a day's work, isn't it? And I'm sure Belinda will take good care of me.' He was quite unaware of the fact that his face revealed that he had been bowled over by Amy's pretty sister.

Amy, trying to save Max's feelings, if they needed to be saved, and hoping he had not noticed the intensity of Gerry's look, said quickly, rather breathlessly, 'Well, that's fine, I'll be happy to go with you to the hospital.' She flashed Max a smile.

'Wonderful,' he said softly, and to her surprise momentarily covered her hand with his. 'You lovely, generous girl.'

'Don't forget to collect the children from school,' Amy instructed Belinda, her muddled thoughts making her sound severe. 'The rehearsal for the play should be over soon.'

Belinda assured her, pushing back a straying golden curl from her forehead, 'Of course I won't forget. Gerry and I will collect them on our way home.'

'Then if you feel up to it, young man, I think we should get moving,' said Max to Richard.

'Yes, I'm much better, thanks. In fact I really could go home—my mum does worry so.'

Max helped him to his feet and patted his shoulder. 'Sorry, old chap, but Dr Grey insists that you go to hospital for a check-up, and I promised I'd see you safely there.'

Amy gave a little laugh and took Richard's arm. 'The powers that be have spoken,' she said jokingly. 'I think we must do as ordered.'

Richard responded bravely with a grin.

'They who must be obeyed,' he said.

'You make Dr Grey and me sound like tyrants,' said Max, assuming a hurt voice.

'So?' queried Amy, bold because her patient was looking less tense and enjoying the badinage. 'What's new?'

'In the car,' answered Max pretending to be fierce. 'Before I lose my cool.'

He helped Richard into the back of the vehicle, and Amy got in beside him. She collapsed gratefully on to the comfortable leather seat. It had been quite a busy afternoon one way and another, both emotionally and physically. She tucked the tartan rug that Max handed her round Richard, who was now, after his efforts at cheerfulness and dismissal of his condition, looking drawn and exhausted.

'Doze off if you want to,' she said, putting an arm round his shoulders.

'I don't think I can, although I feel tired,' he sighed. 'I keep wondering what would have happened if I'd collapsed anywhere else, and you and the doctors hadn't been around to look after me. I might have died!'

'Well, you might well have slipped into a deep coma, and that might have resulted in some lasting damage.'

'Funny, isn't it? I wouldn't carry anything with me to say that I was diabetic, or have a sugar lump in my pocket. I didn't think it would ever happen to me.'

'And will you in the future?' asked Amy.

'You bet I will, even if some of the blokes at school think I'm a weirdo.'

'Is that why you've been stubborn about not taking precautions?'

'Partly that, and partly because I didn't think I'd ever get into difficulties. And Mum worries so much that when I went for a check-up last time I told her I was cured, except that I mustn't have sugar. It cheered her up like anything.'

'And she stopped worrying about your diet and having meals on time!'

Richard said hesitantly, 'Well, she's not always up to cooking or anything, not since she's been ill.'

'Who does the cooking, Richard, when she's not well enough—your father, or are you a dab hand in the kitchen?' Amy asked.

'My dad's gone, he left last year when Mum started to get ill. He just went.' Richard's voice was tight with anger and hurt.

Amy was furious with herself for mentioning his father, though of course she had no means of knowing what had happened.

Max had obviously heard their conversation. He said,

his voice deep and reassuring. 'Sometimes an emergency like this can change things for the better, Rick. We'll have to make sure your mother understands the situation, but I can assure you it will be better in the long run. Mums tend to be tough, you know, where their children are concerned. She'll cope, and I'm certain the cooking business can be sorted out. You just concentrate on keeping fit.'

They pulled up at some traffic lights on the outskirts of the town.

Max turned to look at them both in the back. He grinned. 'Amy,' he suggested, 'why don't you exchange Rick's rather piratical headgear for something more conventional? You'll find a bandage and sterile pad in my case.'

Amy made the necessary exchange as they continued towards the hospital. He doesn't miss a trick, she thought—fancy him noticing that!

In the casualty department they were given VIP treatment. Apparently Dr Grey had rung the senior registrar on duty and warned him of their arrival. It helped that there was apparently a lull in emergencies and accidents, which, the casualty sister assured them, would come to an end as Saturday night revellers and returning football fans filled the streets.

To Amy it seemed odd that this small, quiet cathedral city, with its elegant old buildings and air of restrained gentility, should be subject to the same stresses as the bigger and more violent cities.

Richard was led away to be examined in a cubicle and Max and Amy were asked to wait in a small room off the main reception area. They were offered tea or coffee, and both opted for the former, which was brought to them by a mature auxiliary nurse.

They swallowed the almost tasteless liquid that the

machine had dispensed, and made a face at each other, then laughed.

'I should like to throttle whoever invented these dreadful vending machines,' said Max. 'What a disservice to mankind!'

'Yes,' Amy agreed, turning away to stare out of the window into the darkness. She was suddenly very aware of Max and the fact that they were, for a short while, alone. The memory of the strange look that he had given her over Rick's collapsed form returned forcibly. What had it meant? His eyes had seemed to be full of. . .yes, love. . .but that couldn't be, surely he was in love with Belinda, and Gerry had turned up on the scene, and he and Belinda had. . .

Max was standing behind her. He put a hand on her shoulder and squeezed it gently. 'Amy?' the tone of his voice held a question mark. 'My dear, come back from wherever you went.' He smiled, a kindly, understanding smile.

She turned to look at him and her eyes fastened on the unbuttoned collar of his shirt, where, until he had told her to use it as a bandage, his elegant silk cravat had filled the now open V. There were tiny curly hairs nestling against his throat and disappearing beneath the fine woollen seams of his blue shirt. They were mostly black, but an occasional silver-grey hair curved like a question mark amongst thick clusters. He smelt of some sharp cologne, almost a tweedy scent to match the flecked pattern of his jacket.

She had thought, when he was delivering his opening speech, how virile and immaculate he had looked, properly attired for an Elizabethan Fair, in cavalry twill tailored trousers, sporty jacket and silk cravat. A modern Elizabethan, but one who wouldn't have disgraced the first Elizabeth's court in showy, Tudor garb, with his steely grey eyes and lean chiselled features.

Her heart beat a violent tattoo against her rib cage as Max's hands slid down from her shoulders and round her waist. He gathered her into his arms and gently pressed her head to his chest.

'Amy,' he murmured, his voice thick and very deep, 'I'm so sorry, my love, about Gerry. If I can help, let me know. I'll always be around for you.'

She raised her head and looked at him in bewilderment.

'I don't. . .'

They both heard the door being opened and moved apart. The senior registrar entered.

'Well, we've decided to let young Rick home for the weekend,' he told them. 'He's promised to come in on Monday for the diabetic clinic. Meanwhile, we've given him a diet and insulin guide to use between now and then. He knows that if he gets into difficulties he can come in any time, but if he sticks to his chart he should be OK for the next couple of days.'

'Thank you, Doctor,' said Max formally. 'We'll make sure he attends the clinic on Monday.'

'Right. Thanks for bringing him in.' The tired-looking registrar produced a smile. 'Not your patient, I understand,' he said to Max. 'Good of you to take the trouble.' He smiled at Amy too, before he led the way from the room.

They had to wait a few more minutes before Rick appeared, but they were now in the main reception area which was beginning to fill up with early evening casualties. Amy realised what the A and E sister had meant when she spoke of getting busier as Saturday-night revellers got going.

To Amy it was a relief not to be alone with Max in

private or in a confined space. His words, just before
the casualty doctor had arrived, puzzled her, and she
wanted time to digest them, and to recover from being
held in Max's arms.

It was almost as though he was trying to comfort her,
when, if it was still relevant, she should be comforting
him, on account of what had happened between Belinda
and Gerry Love. But what made Max think that she,
Amy, needed comforting? He didn't, couldn't know of
her love for him, and if he did, surely he would not be
so insensitive as to comment on it in that patronising
fashion and in those circumstances?

No, there was some other reason for his gentle concern, and she must discover what it was and act on it if
possible.

She had just reached this decision, while making
totally banal remarks as they waited for Richard, when
the boy appeared. It was a relief to talk to him, and
hear in detail what the doctor had advised that he
should do to control his diabetes. He seemed to be quite
proud of his chart, which he intended putting up on the
wall of his bedroom so that, as he put it, 'I'm not
tempted to play about with my diet or medication.'

As they got back into the Range Rover, Max having
this time indicated that Amy should join him in the
front of the vehicle, Rick told them he was going to get
a copy made of the chart and pin it up in the kitchen
too.

'Mum will like that,' he said. 'Now that she's a bit
deaf, she likes to be able to see things plainly. I think
she'll enjoy working to a schedule. It'll be like going
back to school for her—she was a teacher, you see, and
is used to timetables and things.'

CHAPTER ELEVEN

As THEY drove back to Monkton through the moonlit frosty lanes, Amy forced herself to listen to Richard and set aside her own thoughts. She had the feeling that Max was doing exactly the same thing. If you listen to people long enough, she thought, you'll find out what makes them, or their environment, tick.

And that was precisely what was happening now. It became apparent, as Richard talked, that he was devoted to his mother, who was ill and had been deserted by her husband. Clearly Rick saw himself as the man of the house and had tried to protect his mother from anything that might add to her distress. It sounded, from what he said, that Mrs Dent was suffering from multiple sclerosis and in addition was rather deaf, and perhaps, understandably, rather sorry for herself.

She had had the telephone removed because she couldn't hear properly, and had become virtually housebound over the last year.

It was surprising to learn that problems of this kind could exist in a close-knit community like Monkton, and that they could remain hidden. Surely there would be any number of people willing and able to help when the need became known? It looked as if the Dents had opted for secrecy about their problem.

Amy caught Max looking at her sideways as they had waited for a car to come out of a side turning. He raised his eyebrows in a quizzical fashion, and she surmised that he was thinking along much the same lines.

'Oh, Kev's here,' said Richard, a note of relief in his voice as they reached his house. 'That's his bike—isn't it great?'

Inside the small front garden, leaning against the privet hedge and hung about with a variety of chains and padlocks, was a very smart racing bicycle.

'Well, well!' said Max, stopping to admire the machine in the light streaming through the glass-panelled front door. 'Quite a fitness freak, your friend— these take some handling.'

'Kev's a great racer.' Rick's small, nondescript face lit up, and his narrow shoulders seemed to widen. 'I'm his timer,' he added proudly.

Amy was pleased to see that this discussion about his friend had virtually completed his recovery from his collapse. Her eyes met Max's over the boy's head and she realised that his interest in the bike, though probably genuine, had also been contrived to give Rick a chance to regain his confidence before going into the house. Another instance of his concern and attention to detail.

This was further underlined when they were introduced to Mrs Dent and Kevin, both of whom showed loving anxiety for Rick's welfare. Mrs Dent was inclined to be helpless and tearful, a condition that Max set about turning to advantage immediately.

'Perhaps you could make us all a cup of tea, Mrs Dent,' he suggested. 'We had some of that filthy stuff like washing-up water that they serve out of those awful machines at the hospital, but we could do with a proper cup.'

For a moment Rick's mother looked as if she was about to refuse, and Kevin half rose to intervene. Obviously quite at home in the Dent household, he would have performed this task, but Max, with an almost imperceptible movement of his hand, prevented him.

'I'll give you a hand, Mrs Dent,' he said, offering her an arm as she struggled out of her chair and picked up a walking stick. Over his shoulder he said, 'Rick, you fill Kevin in on the events of the afternoon, and show him your chart. If he's as good a mate as you say, he'll make sure you stick to it, and Nurse Kincaid will keep a watching brief.' He smiled at the three of them, his eyes lingering on Amy as he escorted Mrs Dent to the kitchen.

The two boys began a lively discussion, with Rick spreading out his chart for Kevin to examine. They were so different—Rick thin, bespectacled, yet very animated and talkative, his friend Kevin muscular and good-looking in a brawny sort of way, not dull, but altogether a slower, more deliberate person than Rick.

Amy, still under the spell of her early morning euphoria and the extraordinary events of the afternoon, which had triggered off the kind of thoughts that dreams are made of, dragged her mind back to the present.

'Are you at school together?' she asked during a lull in the boy's chatter.

'I've just left,' Kevin told her. 'Just started work at Halfords. I was lucky really to get the job with a good cycle firm. There isn't a lot of work around at the moment.'

'He wasn't lucky,' said Rick. 'The manager there is interested in racing and had seen Kev at the junior meets doing his stuff.'

Kevin went scarlet and lightly punched his friend's shoulder. 'Well, it helped,' he said.

Max, carrying a tray with steaming mugs and a plateful of biscuits, returned, followed slowly by Mrs

Dent. It was plain that she had been crying, though she seemed quite in control now.

'Doctor's told me you're not as well as you led me to believe, Rick,' she said, trying to sound severe, but spoiling the effect by ruffling his hair as she passed him.

'Oh, Mum!' he muttered, looking embarrassed.

'You've been over-protective and I've been too sorry for myself. We're going to get things sorted out, starting on Monday. We're going to get the phone put back in, with a special hearing device attached, and get the kitchen altered so I can manage in it as long as possible. That'll do to be going on with, won't it?' She smiled at her son, holding back the tears.

'Oh, Mum!' Rick repeated.

They made some sort of small talk after that, and Amy and Max drank their tea scalding hot. They had done their bit for afternoon. They said goodnight and left as soon as they decently could, the grateful thanks of the Dents and Kevin ringing in their ears.

Silently Max escorted Amy round the Range Rover to the passenger side, unlocked the door and stood by as she climbed in. The bright moonlight silvered the grey in his hair and threw his strong features into relief. He leaned across her and reached for her seat-belt.

Amy held her breath. Her mind was in turmoil. The last quarter of an hour in the Dents' house had been uncomfortable for her. She had never been so conscious of Max's presence and his air of authority, his control over the situation. He had been friendly and helpful, without being pushy or overstepping the professional boundaries of medical etiquette. After all, Rick was Elliot Grey's patient, and Max never forgot it or allowed it to be forgotten.

Somehow, though, underneath the professional con-

cern for a patient, Amy had the feeling that now that
the emergency was over Max's attention was not wholly
absorbed by the Dents and their problem. Several times
she had caught him looking at her, an expression in his
eyes that she could not fathom. Now, the thought of
being alone with him even for the few minutes that it
would take them to drive across the village to the Green
made her feel on edge.

She was still floating on cloud nine, but her usual
practical self was beginning to surface. Everything—
well, nearly everything that had happened that day, she
acknowledged, had been coloured by her own thoughts,
second thoughts in most instances, concerning Max and
Belinda and Gerry.

Perhaps they were no more valid than her original
thoughts had been; maybe they too were a figment of
her imagination and just as wrong. No, she was only
telling herself that, because the second thoughts were so
wonderful, opening up new possibilities. Over the last
few years her expectations of personal happiness had
reached an all-time low. Now she was afraid to hope for
so much that seemed almost within her grasp.

If she was not wrong, Max was not in love with
Belinda, but interested in her, Amy. Once she began to
look at the various happenings over the last month or so
from a totally different angle, many puzzling incidents
made sense.

His coming in daily when she was ill, having her car
repaired, and more done to it, though she couldn't prove
it, than any insurance warranted. His anguished voice
when he'd found her at the scene of the accident, and
the comforting embrace he had given her. His gentle
tenderness on many occasions demonstrated by a
squeeze of hand or arm, or a featherlight kiss on cheek
or brow—or nose, she thought, smiling into the dark-

ness, reliving the moment when he had kissed her this morning.

It had been easy to accept them as signs of filial affection because he intended to marry Belinda, but now—now that she was enlightened, surely they could be interpreted as signs that he was interested in her herself? Perhaps more than interested?

In me, sang the voice in her head exultantly. Max is interested in me!

She felt dreadfully silly, letting her imagination roam so far, and the words had sounded so strong in her head that for a moment she wondered if she had sung them aloud. She must get a grip on herself. She blew her nose hard and peered out of the window at the night sky.

Max spoke suddenly, making her jump. She hadn't realised that he was sitting in the driver's seat and was leaning over to speak to her. His warm breath fanned her earlobe, and she stiffened, determined not to be rattled by his nearness.

'The silence, one might say, is pregnant with unspoken thoughts.'

'I'm sorry—yes, I—I was thinking.' Amy scrabbled around for inspiration. He mustn't guess at her real thoughts. 'I was wondering about the Dents, how they could be helped without being too obvious.' He had started the engine and was fastening his seat-belt. She glanced sideways at him and was glad that in the dimness she wouldn't have to face those piercing grey eyes. 'I'm surprised they haven't been offered a home help, even once a week.'

'I think you'll find that Mrs Dent has turned down all offers of help. Her sort of pride is both understandable and admirable, but in this context a dangerous attribute. Fortunately, today's emergency will probably help her to be more amenable.

'Yes, let's hope so. You were obviously able to persuade her to look at things in a different light while you were helping her to make tea. Did she find it very difficult, by the way, managing the kettle and so on? It was to assess her ability that you insisted on her making tea, wasn't it?'

'So you sussed me out—clever Nurse Kincaid!' He turned to grin at her as they pulled up outside the Doll's House. 'Yes, that was one reason, and to fill her in about young Rick. She's pretty shaky with anything heavy, but I think that's partly lack of confidence. As she said, her son has been spoiling her, and she hasn't even tried to retain some basic skills. Let's hope matters will now improve and she'll not only accept help, but ask for it.'

Amy fumbled to undo her seat-belt, suddenly aware that, with the engine off, the car was very quiet and they were cocooned in the dark interior. The village green had acquired another layer of frost and sparkled under the pale moonlight. It was deserted. The cottages and the other grander properties dotted around displayed discreetly glowing windows. Strangely, this sign of life nearby served only to emphasise their isolation.

'Here, let me.' Max's hand closed over hers as she struggled to release the catch of her belt. He snapped open the metal buckle with sure fingers and eased the webbing from her shoulder.

'Thanks,' she said.

'My pleasure.'

She put her hand on the door-handle, but his hand closed again over hers.

'Wait, Amy, we need to talk.'

'Talk?' she queried.

'Yes—open one's mouth and make intelligent noises with lips and tongue.'

He wasn't being sarcastic, she realised, just trying to lighten the moment, make it easy for her. Not that it did, she couldn't understand why he was so concerned on her account. Like yesterday in the clinic when he had talked about having fun, and younger men, and insisting that she went to fetch Gerry's patient. He had stressed that she should take her time when collecting Mr Steel; even Gerry had remarked on the fact. Surely he couldn't think there was anything between her and Gerry just because she had invited the younger doctor to tea?

On the other hand, he had been quite different this morning when he had arrived at the cottage full of a joyous bonhomie. But this evening at the hospital and at the Dents', after seeing Gerry at the Fair, he had changed again—had seemed protective and kind, rather than. . . Her mind was in an absolute whirl, darting from one possibility to another.

Her lips felt stiff. With difficulty she said, 'Look, it's getting late,' she gestured towards the pink glow of the cottage windows. 'The children ought to be in bed.'

Max looked at the clock on the dashboard and compared it with his wristwatch. 'Yes, you're right, it's after nine. Where has the evening gone?'

Amy's lips unfroze. 'With you looking after somebody else's patient,' she said softly.

'And what about you, Nurse Amy Kincaid—haven't you given up your precious time off to help those who need it most?'

She could feel herself blushing. 'That's not fair,' she said. 'Any nurse. . .'

'Any doctor. . .' he countered.

She forced a laugh. 'Shall we call it quits?'

'Why not?' he said softly, and his hand, which was still on hers, tightened. 'Amy, we must talk,' he repeated. 'But you're right, now's not the time or the place. Can we arrange a meeting with no interruptions from patients, families or friends?'

She felt a wave of panic sweep over her. The euphoria of the morning still weaved about her, but hazily, almost without substance, as if it might be blown away at any moment. The idea of meeting Max on a one-to-one basis was both exhilarating and heart-stopping. Well, she thought, remembering a long-ago school performance of *Macbeth*, 'If it were done when 'tis done, then 'twere well it were done quickly.'

'It won't be easy, but perhaps tomorrow?'

Max groaned. 'Sorry, tomorrow's out. I'm taking the children to see their maternal grandparents in Oxford. By the time we get back it'll be the first Advent service and you and I will be caught up in the choir, and afterwards it will be almost impossible to be alone.'

'Monday?' she queried.

'Oh, Amy, isn't it perfectly bloody—I'm assisting with some chest surgery at the special unit, and that's likely to go on till well into the evening. What about after the clinic on Tuesday? It might be late when we finish, but at least we'll be together, and we can go somewhere to have a meal.'

'I'll have to make sure that Belinda can get home in time to collect Jenny from school.' She glanced at him, still not trusting her creative thoughts about where his interests lay, to see if saying her sister's name upset him, but he remained impassive.

'Well, if she can't and there's a problem let me know. Mrs Carter can collect her and give her tea, as she has in the past with my two. They'll all be delighted.'

Amy felt the first flutterings of unease. It had been acceptable to receive favours from Max when he and Belinda appeared to be on the verge of an understanding, but now that Gerry Love had come between them and she wasn't sure of Max's intentions, was it right to accept help from him?

Unsure of herself, she said more sharply than she meant to, 'That won't be necessary. If Belinda can't get home in time, Miss Treacher, our next-door neighbour, will keep an eye on Jenny.'

Max reached up and switched on the interior light, and turned to face her so that she was forced to look at him.

'I don't know what's wrong between us, Amy,' he said, looking straight into her eyes. 'But I do know that Jenny is important to my children and to Rose in particular. Whatever course we adults, with our supposed superiority, have decided to take, don't let's spoil the children's innocent pleasure in each other's company.'

With a tremendous effort, Amy got a grip on herself. Max was right—why should their problems, or Belinda's defection, tarnish the friendship that existed between his children and her little sister? They all needed each other, and even though Rose's need was obvious because of her deafness, it didn't mean that Jenny didn't need her and Harry. They were the brother and sister of her own generation that she couldn't have. And Harry—he needed someone in whom to confide who wasn't handicapped and in need of protection, and Jenny was that someone.

She regretted her sharp words implying that she didn't need his help with Jenny. They must have sounded sulky and childish. She said, trying to disengage her hands from his, 'You're right, the children are important, we mustn't do anything to upset them.'

'Good, I'm glad you appreciate that. I don't intend failing my children a second time, and our happiness reflects on them, both short-term and long-term. A fractious relationship on whatever level must be avoided at all costs, don't you agree?'

'Yes, of course.' Amy felt small and mean. Whatever else one might think of Max, he couldn't be faulted as a father.

'Right, then, shall we say Tuesday night after work, and to make sure that there are no hiccups I'll ask Mrs Carter to bring Jenny home from school. Belinda can collect her when she gets home, and you won't have to worry at all.' Max looked hard into Amy's eyes, his own expressionless, his voice matter-of-fact. 'It's about time you had someone with whom you can share responsibility, Amy. Single parenting is no picnic—we both know that.' He let her hands go then and started to unlatch his door. 'Don't be too sad about Gerry, my dear. I've a feeling that everything's going to come right in the end, and it's got to be better for Belinda, hasn't it, falling for a younger man.' He switched off the interior light and got out of the car.

Amy gaped into the darkness, trying to take in what he had said. Older man, younger man? That was what he'd said in the clinic yesterday, but then it had seemed to relate to her. Now he was talking about Belinda. Could it mean that her sister had been keen on him but he had not been interested in her, or the other way around?

'Amy—come on, my dear, hop out.' Max stood by the door, hand outstretched. 'It's damn cold!' In the half-light of the moon she could see that he was smiling at her, but she couldn't see whether the smile reached his eyes. He sounded friendly enough, but only friendly, nothing more.

She swung her legs out, but stayed sitting on the side of the high seat. She was frozen, but not with cold. Her mind seemed to have come to a standstill, and it was affecting the rest of her. There was so much that she didn't understand. Why did Max seem to alter his attitude towards her from one moment to the next?

'I'm so muddled,' she grumbled, swallowing a tremble in her throat. 'You and Belinda, older men, younger men—what on earth do you mean?' She shivered.

'You'd better come down.' Max put his hands round her waist and lifted her down. He sounded, she thought, slightly irritated and impatient.

She tilted her head back so that she could look at his face in the moonlight. It bore the impassive expresson that the staff at St Anne's thought was arrogant. 'Max, you said about not minding about Gerry. Well, I don't, much. He's fun, but he's. . .' She nearly said, 'not you,' but held back. 'He's very young—in his way, I mean.'

'And you're so mature? Good try, my dear.' The tone of his voice nearly threw her; it was hard, sarcastic, unbelieving. 'And you *say* you prefer older men, is that it?'

'Yes.' The brevity of her reply concealed a sudden desire to tell him that there was one older man in particular whom she preferred.

Max stared down at her in silence and for one awful moment she thought he had read her thoughts. And if he had, how would he react to that? Would he be flattered, or would he resent her reference, even in thought, to age? He could make comments on it, but could she?

Before she could make up her mind on this, or Max's reaction, the front door of the Doll's House was thrown open. Light streamed out, and Gerry and Belinda stood silhouetted in the doorway.

Max swore savagely and removed his hands from around Amy's waist, but kept a hand beneath her elbow.

Gerry and Belinda were oblivious to them or anything else. They were absorbed in each other, and though standing about a foot apart, looked as if they were going to fall into each other's arms at any moment.

Max gave a wolfish grin. 'Evening,' he called, and his voice and attitude betrayed his feelings. How he must resent Gerry, thought Amy, suddenly arriving on the scene and whipping Belinda from him.

At the sound of Max's voice, Gerry sprang away from Belinda, almost falling down the shallow steps.

Max's nasty grin broadened. 'Call-out?' he asked.

Gerry, very red and embarrassed, replied, 'Yes, but I'm lucky, the first this evening.' He half turned back to Belinda. 'Tomorrow,' he murmured. 'I'll ring tomorrow.'

'Yes, please,' breathed Belinda.

She looked radiant standing in the doorway, wearing a soft woolly sweater, many times too large, in muted shades of purple and bright pink, over patchy pre-shrunk jeans.

'You two coming in?' she asked, and, with a final wave to Gerry as he moved off in his old Triumph Sport, disappeared into the cottage.

Max looked down at Amy and pulled a face. Was he sad, angry, distressed? She had no idea.

He shrugged. 'Till Tuesday, then,' he said in a flat voice.

'Yes.' She felt churned up with various emotions, but tried to make her face as unreadable as his.

They went through the tiny hall to the kitchen.

'Coffee?' asked Amy.

'Please.' Max perched himself on the side of the table while she poured coffee from the percolator. He didn't say anything, just watched her, and grinned when she blushed and spilt some coffee as she handed him his mug. Amy wondered why he hadn't followed Belinda into the sitting-room. It was obvious that that was where he wanted to be.

'Ah,' he said, to her surprise, 'the cool Nurse Kincaid can be ruffled!' He gave her a quirky smile, then muttered softly, 'Amy—oh, Amy!' in a sad, thoughtful manner.

It wasn't surprising that he was sad; he was bound to be, on account of seeing Gerry with Belinda. He must have been dreading that something like this would happen, perhaps certain, at his most rational, that he would lose Belinda to a younger man at some point. It could partly explain his recent words and actions where she was concerned, Amy thought, when perhaps being close to her was the next best thing to being close to Belinda. How could she have thought otherwise? Nothing had changed; how could Max be seriously interested in her when her lovely sister was around?

She sighed loudly without meaning to, and swallowed a lump of pain and something like humiliation. Her first thoughts about Belinda and Max had been accurate. It was Belinda he fancied like mad, and if she, Amy, figured in his thoughts to any degree, it was quite definitely as a useful second best.

Max looked at her sharply. 'Are you all right?' he asked.

'I'm fine,' said Amy firmly. 'Let's go and see what the others are doing.' She led the way back into the sitting-room.

Belinda and Jenny and Rose and Harry stood at the casement window overlooking the Green.

There was an excited shout from the four of them, as Max and Amy entered. 'It's snowing!' called Harry. 'Come and look, it's actually snowing!'

'A white Christmas, perhaps,' said Max as he and

Amy joined the others at the window. 'A good omen, do you think?'

'Oh yes, definitely,' Amy agreed, gathering all her courage to sound normal, and remembering the conversation she had had with Jenny that morning about the snow in November. 'A good omen.' Silently wondering, for whom, for what?

Max took his two tired and excited children home soon afterwards. Amy, standing with her sisters in the doorway of the Doll's House to wave goodbye, wondered if anything would come of the aborted conversation that she and Max had started. Omens. Had it been, she wondered, a good or bad omen that had interrupted them just when they were beginning to exchange confidences? What would he have said that might have altered the evening, even the direction of their lives, that the sight of Gerry and Belinda together had made it impossible for him to divulge?

Only time would tell. She felt drained, empty, but she put on a show for Belinda and Jenny, both so content with their happy day.

Somehow she held back the tears until she was safe in her own bed.

Amy didn't expect to have any contact with Max until Sunday evening, when they would meet in church. It was therefore unexpected, and a little unnerving, when the phone rang just after eight o'clock on Sunday morning, and Belinda, who had hurried to pick it up, no doubt hoping it was Gerry, handed her the receiver.

'For you,' she said with a grin. 'Lover boy.' She rolled her eyes and puckered her lips into a kiss.

'Who?' Amy kept her hand over the mouthpiece, genuinely puzzled.

'Dr Max Bentley, who else? Don't tell me you're just

good friends. Didn't look that way last night. I thought he was absolutely smouldering!'

How on earth could she think that? wondered Amy, and mouthed at her, 'Don't talk rot,' and then into the telephone in a cool voice, 'Good morning, Max, I thought you'd be on your way to Oxford by now.'

Belinda grinned and went through to the kitchen.

'We're just starting out,' said Max.

'Oh.' She couldn't think of anything to say. Why on earth had he phoned?

'I'm sorry things just fizzled out last night in such a frustrating fashion.'

'Yes, I'm sorry too.' Her voice wavered a bit.

'You don't sound very certain,' he commented.

'Oh, but I am.'

'Looking forward to Tuesday night?'

Was she? She didn't know.

'Very much.' She tried to infuse some warmth into her voice.

'Good. I'd better go now, see you tonight in church. Goodbye.'

'Goodbye, have a safe journey.'

Amy stood in the hall after she had replaced the receiver, wondering why Max had bothered to phone. Had he in fact wanted to talk to Belinda? Just to hear her voice, perhaps. Such a thing might happen to anyone hopelessly in love, especially with a much younger woman who had made it obvious that she'd fallen for someone else.

Had he always known that his infatuation with Belinda was hopeless, could that account for some of his generosity towards herself? Amy sat on the bottom stair and tried to think things through. That Max was genuinely fond of her, she didn't doubt, but then he was equally fond of Jenny. A cynical thought came unbid-

den—she and Jenny had their value to Max, she as a
stand-in mother for his children, and Jenny as a devoted
friend to both Rose and Harry.

Well, it was fine by her that he should put his
children's wellbeing first, but why had he muddied the
waters, so to speak, by pursuing Belinda in the first
place? Had he been so beguiled by her that he hadn't
seen through her pose as a capable, dedicated help to
her younger sister? Could she blame him if he had been
taken in by her beautiful sister, as so many men had
before him? No, she couldn't; she just wished he hadn't
confused matters by being at times so nice to her, saying
and doing things that were open to misinterpretation.
Or perhaps—there was a thought—because her own
heart was so vulnerable, only she could misinterpret
them.

Everything was so uncertain. Just when she had
begun to feel that life was getting better and better, why
the hell did things have to get so complicated? Given
time she might even have come to terms with the fact
that Max was in love with Belinda, learned to live with
it. But Gerry had come on the scene, and Belinda had
fallen for him like a ton of bricks. Max didn't stand a
chance, and, knowing it, was maybe hedging his bets.
That sounded dreadful, calculating, but might he have
decided that Kincaids mark two and three were better
than no Kincaids at all? Given his protective love for his
children, it was possible.

He was an intelligent and sophisticated man and a
splendid doctor. Perhaps the amalgam of all these
attributes made it possible for him to put his emotions
in cold storage and seek an alternative solution to his
problems.

Amy mentally shook herself. Whatever was she thinking about? Compromise, of course, she answered herself

calmly; he would compromise for the sake of his children. He would turn his back on a passionate, hopeless love match with Belinda, in favour of a steady, low-key, loving relationship with her accommodating self—good, plain old Amy, who would make a dutiful wife, and an affectionate stepmother.

She felt her lips compress into a thin line. 'Well,' she muttered furiously, 'we'll see about that, Dr Max Bentley!'

CHAPTER TWELVE

THE morning drifted away. The three of them attended the eleven o'clock sung Eucharist, then hurried home from church through the grey late morning to lunch, crunching over the thin layer of snow.

Belinda was on great form, full of her own kind of quirky humour because Gerry had phoned just before they'd left the house. Jenny loved her in this mood, treating her as she would a friend of her own age, and Belinda was quick to respond. Watching the two of them throw ill-made snowballs at each other, Amy was happy for them, though consumed by the bitter thoughts and the conclusions she had reached concerning Max. They lay like lead in her heart and mind.

She recalled how she and Jenny had walked home across the Green under the stars in October. A sense of belonging to this pretty Sussex village had been strong then, and was still strong, in spite of the now fragile links with the Bentleys.

She had put a casserole into the oven before they left, to have with jacket potatoes and cheese. The kitchen smelt delightfully aromatic as they let themselves into the Doll's House.

Amy and Belinda had a glass of sherry while they were setting the table, and Jenny had a ginger beer.

'I say,' she remarked as Belinda filled her glass, 'do you know this is two per cent alcoholic?'

'It's quite safe for you to drink,' confirmed Amy.

'Oh, I know that. When I was at the Bentleys' I drank low-alcohol or alcohol-free wine, and Dr Max drank it when he was on call. I think we should keep some in house.'

'The Oracle has spoken,' said Belinda with a laugh. 'What about it, then, Amy—shall we get some in for our two medics to imbibe when they're on call?'

Amy, busy dishing up the meal, wondered how Belinda could possibly be blind or indifferent to Max's feelings. Or was she? 'Our two medics' had a nice ring to it. If only it were true. Unlikely considering the way things were shaping, but one could pretend. 'Brilliant idea,' she agreed.

The front doorbell rang at that moment, and Jenny hurried to answer it.

Belinda said, 'I'm starving, I hope it isn't someone who's going to stop us eating.' It was amazing how she remained wand-slim, yet ate like the proverbial horse.

Miss Treacher was at the door. Amy and Belinda heard her asking if they were in, and almost at once Jenny, wide-eyed but composed, appeared leading their next-door neighbour into the kitchen.

'Miss Treacher's hurt her arm,' she said calmly. 'I think you should look at it, Amy.'

Amy saw at once what was wrong. Miss Treacher had obviously scalded herself. She was holding her right arm out stiffly in front of her; it was inflamed and beginning to swell. Her thin face was crumpled up with pain.

'Here', said Amy, leading her to the sink. She turned on the tap and guided the injured arm beneath the jet of cold water with one hand, as she put the plug in with the other and the sink began to fill up. 'Stool,' she said briskly to Belinda, and to Jenny, 'First aid box, love, from the bathroom cupboard, please.'

Belinda pushed a high stool underneath Miss Treacher's bottom and gently helped her to perch on it.

'Would it be all right if Miss Treacher had a cup of tea or coffee?' she asked Amy. 'I think she's rather shocked.'

'Good idea—either, with lots of sugar.' Amy gave Miss Treacher a reassuring smile and put a supporting arm round her thin shoulders. She asked jokingly to relieve the tension, 'Has Madam any preferences—tea, coffee, cocoa?' and remembering that the lady was a Scot, 'Even a wee dram is available, though I wouldn't advise it at this moment.'

Miss Treacher managed a shaky smile. 'You're verra kind, but tea would suit me fine. I feel so silly,' she continued, 'letting the steam from the pan go all around my arm. Would you ever know anything so daft!'

'It could happen to anyone, Miss Treacher. At least we've got it under control, I think, though it'll take a little time to cool it down properly.'

Jenny had returned with the first aid box.

'What do you want out of it?' she asked Amy importantly.

'Nothing yet, love. Later on we'll have a clean wide piece of gauze to put over the burn area, and a triangular bandage to make a sling if necessary.'

'A sling?' queried the casualty. 'Does that mean I have to go to the hospital?' For some reason, sling and hospital seemed to be synonymous.

'I shouldn't think so, but you should see your doctor tomorrow so that he can check that there's no infection. I only suggest a sling to make you feel more comfortable, but it may not be necessary.'

In the event, it wasn't. Amy kept the injured arm submerged in cold water, with ice cubes being enthusiastically added by Jenny, for about twenty minutes. Both the inflammation and swelling had by then disappeared. There were two or three small blisters, but nothing alarming. Amy covered the affected area with clean gauze secured by a light bandage.

'Here, take these two Paracetamol tablets,' she suggested. 'And take these with you to have if you have any more pain.' She handed over another six tablets, and, rather embarrassed, received effusive thanks for these, and for her help.

Belinda escorted Miss Treacher to her cottage, down one brick path and up another the other side of the cobbled wall that divided the two gardens. She had refused the Kincaids' offer of lunch, as she had a friend coming for tea.

Returning from the next-door cottage, Belinda, very cheerful and happy in spite of her delayed meal, enquired of Amy if she had done her bit well.

'Will I make a good doctor's wife?' she asked, looking rather wistful. 'I know I've a lot to learn, but I'll work hard at it.'

Amy, dishing up their belated meal, was able to confirm with confidence that her sister had proved herself, while marvelling at the change that falling in love had wrought in Belinda. Not entirely due to Gerry, of course, Belinda's improvement had started earlier, she decided. She would have to ask her about this some time.

Belinda's new-found responsibility, and her seemingly genuine attraction to Gerry, was astonishing. Love at first sight, with Belinda for once as much a victim to her emotions as her beloved.

The rest of the afternoon, foreshortened on account of Miss Treacher's accident, was spent writing Christmas cards.

'Shall we do all those from the three of us that have to be sent by post?' asked Amy.

'Yes, please. Bags I put the stamps on and seal the envelopes,' replied Jenny happily.

'Right, but no licking, don't want you getting a sore throat for Christmas.'

'OK.' Jenny rushed to the kitchen and returned with a saucer full of water.

'I'll do the addresses if you write the cards Amy,' offered Belinda.

'Right. Now, who shall we start with?'

Great-Aunt Megan was the unanimous choice, though they would be visiting her over the Christmas period.

They played carols on the music system as they worked and chatted. It was the first time since their mother had died, Amy realised, that they had worked together so harmoniously on a family chore. And that, of course, was mainly due to Belinda's changed personality.

The phone rang just before five o'clock and Belinda rushed to answer it.

'That was Gerry,' she explained, returning to the sitting-room, looking very flushed and pretty, a few minutes later. 'Somebody's taking over from him at six o'clock, and he'd like to come to Evensong with us and then carol-singing afterwards.' She looked rather uncertainly at Amy. 'I said to come. Is that all right?'

'Of course—it'll be lovely. Look, let's have our tea and crumpets now and I'll pop a macaroni cheese into the oven before we go to church. It'll be ready when we get back, plenty for all of us.'

'Oh, yes, for Max and the children too. Shall I make a tossed salad? That would be nice with it.'

'Great,' agreed Amy.

'And I,' said Jenny, not to be outdone, 'will make up my special mayonnaise to go with the salad, and put out nuts and crisps and things.'

Amy, already toasting crumpets between the wire rack of the Aga, found it hard to keep up a front in the face of her sisters' concerted happiness, which seemed to be making a mockery of her own loveless condition.

They all arrived at the church porch together, Gerry and the Kincaids, and the Bentleys. Max seemed, in a restrained fashion, pleased to see them, while the children were bursting with delight at being together again, as if they had been separated for years, not hours. Max caught Amy's eye and raised a humorous, quizzical brow at the children's noisy reunion. To her surprise, and a mixture of resentment and pleasure, Max placed a hand beneath her elbow as they ascended the stairs to the choir loft.

The service was magical, the church beautifully decorated with late golden chrysanthemums and yellow and green variegated holly, and a forest of candles.

Amy felt her spirits lift and some of her bitterness drain away. Against her will, Max's presence affected her, as had the feeling of his hand beneath her elbow. She found herself wondering if loving friendship might be acceptable, if high romance was not on offer. But she found that for the moment she was content.

Happiness, or something akin to it, spilled over into her singing, and into Belinda's. Both lyric sopranos, they sang like angels, soaring easily through the difficult harmonies of 'O Come, O Come, Emmanuel'. While Max, a powerful bass, had to hold himself back so as not to drown out the other singers.

Although they were separated by a dozen or more other choristers, and it was quite ridiculous, but Amy felt as if Max was touching her, so strong were the vibes that he was sending her way. But still she didn't know quite how he felt about her. Affection certainly, but more than that. . . ? She would have to wait until their date on Tuesday to learn more about this distinguished, enigmatic man. Perhaps, after all, he was thinking in terms of protective—almost paternal affection for her and her sisters. Maybe this talk that he wanted to have was about a future for them and their families, rather than one simply between him and her.

Of course, it would have to be on the terms that she had considered, and should reject, that of substitute mother, and by the same token substitute lover. I feel like a teenager in love for the first time, she thought, and sympathised with Belinda over her numerous 'crushes', and the certainty that each time was 'the real thing'.

Well, I at least can be confident that this is the real thing for me, she decided. I'm old enough and practical enough to know my own mind. But can I accept second best? Could I possibly agree to anything less than Max's total devotion? Would being with him and caring for his children be enough? She almost choked on the thought. What made her think he intended making her any sort of offer, a suggestion that they needed to talk? She was letting her imagination run away with her.

The service came to an end, and Amy hovered at her bench ostensibly tidying away hymn-books and sheet music, willing Max to join her. Belinda hurried towards the spiral staircase to join Gerry and the children.

'Won't be long,' said Amy.

'Take your time,' said Belinda with a cheeky grin. 'I'll keep the others happy.'

The innuendo was obvious, and Amy wondered crossly how she could get things so wrong.

The choir loft emptied of everyone save Amy and Max. He strode along the narrow gangway, two steeply rising tiers above her station, then swung long legs over the intervening benches to stand beside her.

There were still many of the congregation below in the body of the church, slowly easing themselves out of pews into the aisle, but the two of them were very much alone beneath the vaulted roof of the bell tower, which rose above the choir.

Max said, 'I've been thinking about you all day.'

'Really?'

He gave her a searching look. 'Really.' He touched her arm, and with difficulty Amy stopped herself from trembling. 'You sound sceptical—as if you don't believe me.'

'I believe you, but I'm still not sure. . .' Her voice trailed away. Whatever she said would reveal her feelings to him, and that she was determined not to do, until he had explained some of the small mysteries of the past weeks.

'Amy——' He looked at her long and hard, his grey eyes glinting with some indefinable emotion, while an altar boy extinguished the candles and the air was filled with the scent of incense mingling with candle grease. 'We'd better go,' he said at last.

'Yes.'

The church had emptied completely before they found their way down the winding iron staircase, through the porch and out on to the gravelled path that encircled the church.

A crocodile of carol-singers was forming up behind the Rector. An occasional snowflake, large and fluffy, fluttered down on to the iron-hard frosted earth below. Everyone was given a lighted taper to hold, and the flames, impervious to the odd flake of snow, burned steadily in the freezing night air.

The column started off on their pilgrimage round the

houses on the outskirts of the village. The choir was now mingling with everyone else, so Max and Amy were able to walk side by side. She was still happy in a vague manner, in spite of matters still being in the air between them, and Max also seemed content. After all, they had Tuesday to look forward to.

Later there would be a last carol sung on the Green, before everyone made for home or the Cricketers for a drink, or, in the case of the Bentleys and Kincaids, to the Doll's House for the rest of the evening.

Somehow the Rector and his wife also returned to the Doll's House for supper. Amy was too busy playing hostess to further indulge in private thoughts and hopes.

Monday seemed a long day. It dragged for Amy, though she was busy on bloods and other specimen tests, and had several difficult patients to deal with. There were two cases of flaccid blood vessels, almost impossible to pressurise sufficiently to draw up enough blood for investigation. It was a small triumph to eventually succeed without causing either patient too much distress. Normally she would have been absorbed in her work and oblivious to time, but on this occasion, she found herself glancing at her fob watch every so often, and wondering what Max was doing.

The pneumonectomy he had told her about, during a brief interlude in the kitchen after the carol service, when they had deliberately avoided personal in favour of professional intimacy, would be well on the way now.

'Excision of a whole lung is serious, requires careful surgery, but is generally straightforward,' Max had explained. 'But in this case there are other problems. The other lung is in pretty poor shape, and the patient generally debilitated and undernourished. The thing is, we can't afford to wait any longer.'

'What are the chances of a successful op?' asked Amy.

'Fifty-fifty at best. Good post-surgical nursing and physio is going to improve the old boy's chances. You'd appreciate that. Of course, the nursing staff at the unit are good, but I wish you were in charge of his recovery, I'd feel much more confident about the outcome.'

'Well, thank you, kind sir,' she smiled, thrilled by the simple sincerity of his remark. To have his professional regard was a small comfort.

Well, that was yesterday. Amy pulled herself together and firmly back into the clinic-room and the sorting of lab forms. She was ashamed of herself, for letting her mind dwell on personal matters when she was on duty. 'Pull yourself together, Kincaid,' she told herself, and by a great effort succeeded.

Not till she was driving home did she consider again her meeting with Max the following day.

Would she be prepared to compromise if he gave her the opportunity to do so? Her mind see-sawed between possible options—bleak years without Max, or a future with him but overshadowed by his love for Belinda. She was filled with self-disgust that she, Amy Kincaid, was even prepared to give the possiblity house-room.

'Love, bloody love—who needs it?' she muttered savagely, and put her foot down hard on the accelerator.

CHAPTER THIRTEEN

TUESDAY—chest clinic day and the joy of working with Max all the afternoon and spending the evening alone with him, was Amy's first thought when she woke in the morning. Then reality hit her, and she recalled with a shiver and a leaden heart the events of the weekend and the probably traumatic day that lay ahead of her.

A thin, pale light filtered through the curtains of her tiny casement window, and when she pulled them back and bent to look out through the diamond panes, it was to discover that another layer of snow had fallen.

The Green was almost untouched, its smooth surface broken only by an occasional clawed pattern where a bird had landed; and scarred by a thin, straight line of paw-marks made by some four-footed animal, travelling from north to south. But there were rut marks on the road where the milk float and several other vehicles had passed.

She heard, before she saw, a car approaching slowly from the south end of the road, and suddenly there was Max drawing up in the Range Rover outside the cottage gate.

He got out of the car and glanced up at her window as if knowing that she was there. Her silly heart, which hadn't yet learned its lesson, thumped with pleasure at the sight of him. He raised a gloved hand in greeting, before unlatching the gate and striding up the garden path.

Amy pulled her old wool dressing-gown over her striped pyjamas and wished she were wearing something more glamorous. It was too late to do anything about it now. She gave her hair one or two vigorous strokes with a brush, squirted on some of her favourite perfume, and tore down the stairs.

'Hi,' she said breathlessly as she opened the door.

'Hi,' returned Max, removing his driving gloves.

There was a creak on the landing above, and Jenny's voice floated down the narrow staircase.

'Amy, are you in the bathroom? I think there's someone at the door, shall I go and answer it?'

'No, it's all right, love, I'm down here already, and it's Dr Max who's called. I'm getting breakfast—you use the bathroom.' Amazingly Amy's voice sounded quite normal.

'Oh, how lovely! Dr Max, hello.' Jenny's shining morning face appeared at the top of the stairs, as Max smiled up at her.

'Hello, Jenny, looking forward to the dress rehearsal for the play this afternoon?'

'Oh, yes! Rose and I look very pretty in our angel dresses.'

'I'm sure you do, poppet. You get ready for school now, I'm going to give Amy a hand in the kitchen.'

'Wow, that's brilliant!' She disappeared and they heard her go into the bathroom.

'I think we'd better make for the kitchen,' suggested Amy, assuming a calm she didn't feel. 'Even Belinda won't have slept through that lot!'

In fact, Belinda appeared moments later, looking tousled and, as always, beautiful.

'Hello, Max, I thought I heard your voice.' She gave him a wide, dimpling smile. 'Come to give me a lift?'

'As needed,' replied Max calmly. 'I know Amy's not on till eleven, so I thought I might offer you my chauffeuring services.'

'Great,' said Belinda. 'Just what I need.'

'I also came,' said Max, 'to remind you that Amy and I are going out for a meal tonight, and Mrs Carter's picking up the three children from school. I'm sure we can rely on you, Belinda, to pick up Jenny later, and see her safely to bed.'

Belinda looked outraged and made as if to say something rude, but he held up his hand to stop her and said, sounding meek, 'Sorry, sorry—I shouldn't question it, but you know what a fusser your big sister is, and we don't want her worrying all the evening, do we? Am I forgiven?'

'OK, you're forgiven,' said Belinda with a laugh.

And what was all that about? Amy asked herself, after Max and Belinda had left. No way had he come here to check up about this evening—that was just an excuse, but an excuse for what? She didn't know. She mulled over possibilities when she was on her way to Castleminster, going by bus, as Max would be driving her home that night, but didn't reach any conclusions. What an unpredictable man he was!

He confounded her again that morning, by unexpectedly arriving in the paediatric department where she had been working since coming on duty.

'Hello, Adam,' he greeted Dr Wilder, the elderly senior paediatrician, 'finished your clinic? May I steal Miss Kincaid away from you so we can snatch a sandwich before getting stuck in this afternoon?'

'Miss Kincaid?' Dr Wilder looked puzzled for a moment. 'Oh, Nurse Amy, that's what the children call her. Of course. I'm sure she's got everything under control, haven't you, Nurse?'

Amy, pink with a mixture of hard work, surprise and pleasure, nodded.

'Yes, all the notes are filed and future appointments noted.'

'Thank you, and many thanks for your help this morning.' Dr Wilder looked at her as if he was seeing her for the first time. 'You know, the children love you—er——' he hesitated '—Amy. That's quite a compliment. Would you be willing, if I put your name forward, to special in this unit?'

Amy gaped at him and looked at Max, astonished to find that she wanted him to answer for her.

'Well, at this moment,' said Max drily, 'I'm sure Amy's only thinking of eating, and the long afternoon in front of her in my clinic.'

'Oh, well, yes, of course,' agreed Dr Wilder, giving them a speculative, intelligent look as they left.

For a moment, as they left St Anne's, Amy thought Max was taking her to lunch because he was going to cry off their evening engagement. But it was nothing of the sort.

'I thought,' he said, 'that lunch together might make a nice appetiser for tonight—don't you agree?'

Now what was he up to? She was puzzled and a bit suspicious, but couldn't help but be pleased.

'Rather—what a lovely idea!' Lunch *and* dinner. In spite of being uncertain about the outcome of either meal spent in Max's company, she felt like a child, already surfeited with goodies, unable to resist another favourite chocolate.

A short while later, as they sat at a table in the Castleminster Arms, with drinks in front of them as they waited for their food, Max said, 'Remember the first time we came here?'

'Yes, I nearly passed out. I had flu.'

'Yes—poor Amy!' He stared at her across the table in the corner of the busy pub. His cool grey eyes mesmerised her. She couldn't look away. She knew that whatever he was going to say, she wouldn't want to hear, and she was right. 'We're in a mess, my dear, aren't we? Caught up in a French farce with each person loving the wrong person.'

She breathed in sharply, surprised by the analogy, and yet admitting to herself that it was as good a way as any to describe the ridiculous muddle they were in. It would be pointless to pretend not to understand what he meant. Was he going to confide in her about his feelings for Belinda? Surely not, it just wasn't his style.

'Yes,' she agreed sadly, 'we are in a mess.' She wanted to add, 'poor Max,' but his aloofness even now made it impossible.

She felt tears stinging her eyes, and lowered her head so that he shouldn't see them. He reached across the table and patted her tightly clasped hands, in a paternal, almost avuncular fashion.

'It must be hell at this moment,' he said quietly. 'But it will get easier as time goes on, and I'll do all I can to help, believe me.'

Amy raised her head and stared at him in disbelief. How arrogant and conceited could he get, she thought, twisting everything round so that he didn't have to admit his unreturned love for Belinda, but could magnanimously offer to help her come to terms with her love for him. She couldn't believe it of him. How could he be so crass, so insensitive; how could he humiliate her so, and all to save his ego?

A waitress arrived with their food. Amy removed her

hands from beneath Max's, smiled sweetly at the waitress and nodded her thanks, then turned a stony face towards Max, and stood up. She leaned across the table and actually hissed at him, 'How dare you, Dr Bentley, how dare you!' And then, stumbling between the crowded tables, she made her way up the stairs as fast as she could.

She heard him calling her name, but didn't pause until she reached the Cathedral Close. The cloisters were usually quiet, but today they were thronged with Christmas shoppers as well as other workers like herself, on a lunch break. Amy squeezed her way round and between leisurely groups, aware that Max was gaining on her. Suddenly his hand was encircling her arm.

'Wait, Amy—wait!' he begged breathlessly.

'Let me go! Don't ever touch me again!'

Max released her with an expletive, but continued to walk with long strides beside her as she tried frantically to put distance between them. She became aware of a noisy disturbance ahead of them, and slowed down.

A bunch of noisy youths came towards them, passing a large transistor from one to the other, forcing everyone they met to move out of their way. An elderly lady walking slowly in front of Max and Amy tried to side-step, but tripped.

Max caught the lady's arm and helped her to one side of the cloister. By then the youths were upon them and Amy was shoved the other way towards the arches opening on to the grass quadrangle.

One of the noisy gang leered at her, and said, ''ello, darling,' in a suggestive manner, and stretched out a hand as if he was going to touch her face. She struck it aside, and, before he could react, slid round the pillar and out of his way.

He slowed down and turned as if to follow her, an

angry expression replacing the leering one of a moment before. Amy was briefly scared, but turned to face him. 'I'll kick you where it hurts most!' she threatened. He realised she meant it, and backed off, mumbling something foul. He joined his mates as they continued on their destructive way, leaving a trail of flustered and sometimes frightened people in their wake.

'Amy! Darling!' she heard Max's voice, anxious, concerned, imperious, as she appeared from behind the pillar. 'Are you all right?'

'Fine.' Her heart thumped—he'd called her 'darling' quite spontaneously. She was suddenly aware of the emotion in his voice.

She was about to join him, since it was obvious that he couldn't yet leave the elderly lady whom he was supporting, when there came a shout from the end of the cloister. It wasn't the gang of youths causing trouble, it came from the opposite direction. In fact, the gang's loud transistor could still be heard, though receding, as they turned the corner from the long cloister.

The shout, a man's shout, was followed by a woman's scream, and then the loud bawling of a child in tears. Amy looked down the passageway and saw a man and a woman and a small child standing in the middle of the cloister.

'Stop him!' shrieked the woman who had screamed. 'He's got my baby!'

The crowd, who had been forced to part when the youths had pushed their way through, were still in the main pressed against the walls of the Cathedral on the one side of the cloister, or against the pillars on the other. They seemed frozen to the spot.

'Stay back!' shouted Max, as Amy started towards the youth. 'He's got a gun!'

There was a loud bang, a whining sound, and a metallic zip, as a bullet scraped along the flint wall.

'Down!' Max's voice rang out again, and Amy saw him push the old lady to the ground and crouch over her.

She crouched too, trying to control her shaking limbs. The sound of the man's feet as he pounded over the paved cloister grew louder as he approached. So did the sound of the child's cries. 'Mummy, Mummy!' he was calling between great bursts of tears.

Head very low, Amy peered out.

The man and the boy, whom he was half dragging, half carrying, were about thirty feet away. She reasoned that he couldn't take proper aim on the run, and would hardly stop to do so. She prepared herself for the moment when man and boy drew level with her pillar.

Just before they reached her, the man let off another shot, and the sounds as she heard them before registered, though not consciously. A bang, a whine, a tearing sound, only this time from above, as the bullet hit the roof.

Again Max shouted at her, but she couldn't hear what he was saying. He was waving his arms up and down. The man and boy were almost level with her now, less than a yard away from the pillar. The child's feet barely touched the ground as he was heaved along. Amy lunged forward and grabbed the boy round his legs. The man didn't stop running, and both she and the boy were dragged over the flagstones a little way, until the gunman realised what was happening.

He turned, still moving, and the hand that held the gun was pointing in her direction, though waving about unsteadily. Out of the corner of her eye, Amy noticed a blurred movement, and saw that it was Max, springing forward, landing on the running man, pushing up the arm that held the gun. She could see the gunman's other hand, holding the boy, slacken.

'Let go!' she shouted in the child's ear, but he was either too frightened to do so, or couldn't hear. She loosed one hand from her hold on his legs and tugged at his arm. Abruptly his small hand slipped from the man's grasp.

Everything went quiet for a moment as they both came to a sudden stop, and the bruising pain of being dragged over the uneven flagstones ceased.

Amy raised her head and saw Max and the gunman rolling over and over, snarling at each other as they both tried to get possession of the gun.

'Max, my darling! Be careful!' She was hardly aware of what she'd shouted, only conscious that Max was in terrible danger.

There was another loud blast, another whine, another long-drawn-out harsh screech as a bullet seared a passage along the granite wall of the Cathedral.

Instinctively Amy flung herself over the little boy. Everything was suddenly silent—not just quiet, but silent. Down the length of the cloister, nobody moved. The two men, a moment before grunting and growling like animals over the gun, were still and silent.

'Max,' Amy whispered, and rolled off the small boy's body.

He whimpered, 'I want my mum!'

'She's coming,' said Amy. 'You stay there.'

She crawled the few feet towards the tangled heap that was Max and the gunman, praying as she went that Max was unhurt. The gun lay some distance away where it had skidded over the flagstones after the last shot.

Her movement seemed to galvanise everyone else into

action. Suddenly there was noise and activity every-where, and people came running from all sides.

She reached the two still forms, almost afraid to breathe, just as Max raised his head. His eyes focused on her, and he managed a half smile, then winced with pain.

'Oh, my darling,' exclaimed Amy, 'are you hurt?'

'No, only winded,' he ground out in a voice tight with pain. And then, very surprised, 'You called me your darling!' His grey eyes bored intently into hers. 'Gerry?' he asked hazily, but before she could speak, put up a hand and touched her cheek. 'You're hurt, dear love, you're hurt!'

'Only a graze.' She didn't care about anything, she wanted to burst out singing or something. 'His dear love', he'd said. He loves me, he loves me! What did anything in the whole wide world matter?

All sound and movement was held in suspense, it was a fraction of a moment, but it might have been hours.

The gunman groaned.

'Help me up, love,' said Max, his voice calm, 'I've twisted my knee.'

'Badly?'

He grimaced. 'Badly enough. No,' he changed his mind, 'I'd better look at him before I get up—safer. I think he may have broken something, possibly his arm.'

He eased himself towards the man and Amy crouched down beside him. The man's gun arm lay stretched out at a peculiar angle, and the face he turned towards them was grey and beaded with sweat.

'You've probably broken your arm, old chap,' said Max sounding like a doctor talking to a patient and not a recent enemy. 'Lie still—the ambulance will be here shortly.' He looked up enquiringly at the circle of people now gathered about them. 'Somebody has phoned for an ambulance, I trust?' His voice was now staccato, sharp.

'Oh, yes,' somebody replied. 'And someone went over to the clinic just across the square, to fetch a doctor. You ought to stay quiet, mate, and let someone medical have a look at you before you move around.'

Max gave Amy a quirky smile. 'Yes, you're probably right. I'll sit tight for a bit.' To Amy he said quietly, 'Go and look at the little boy and his mother. I'm not much good at the moment and I should keep an eye on him,' he nodded towards the gunman. 'I don't want him to move that arm, and I think our friends here might be a little rough with him, given the chance.'

Amy nodded and made her way over to the child and his mother. She didn't really care much what happened now. Max was safe, and he loved her, that was all that mattered.

She didn't understand why everything had seemed such a muddle. It seemed plain enough now that Max loved her and not Belinda, and that he had thought her in love with Gerry, and suffering because Gerry was in love with Belinda. No wonder he had called it a French farce! That was why, of course, Max had offered his help and comfort, from the most generous of motives, to get her through what he saw as the trauma of losing Gerry. And she had thought him egotistical and conceited! How could she? The sooner she could put that matter right and apologise, the better.

It was astonishing how all these thoughts wove in and out of her mind as she knelt down beside the young woman and the small boy, and reassured them.

She was beginning to ache all over now, and became aware of several sore and bleeding spots. It was a great relief when the ambulance arrived, and the crew took over.

CHAPTER FOURTEEN

THEY were given a great welcome when they returned to St Anne's later that afternoon. Their colleagues had attended to their injuries.

Amy's grazed face and hands were treated and Max's knee X-rayed. There was no fracture, but a severe sprain with pulled ligaments was diagnosed, and he was given a painkilling injection and fitted with a support bandage.

They snatched a few minutes' conversation while they were waiting in Max's surgery for Carter to arrive and drive them home. It seemed odd to be sitting there, doing nothing, for once patients themselves.

Max took Amy's hands gently in his. 'Poor little hands,' he said. 'So sore, and you were so brave. Do you know, my darling, what most worried me when the maniac started shooting?'

'No.' They were sitting side by side on the examination couch, adjusted to the lowest level for comfort.

'I hadn't told you I loved—had loved you since that first day when you assisted in the clinic. I thought, if he pots either of us, Amy will never know how much I love her.'

'Oh, Max, I thought like that too. It was agony to think you might be hurt, dead perhaps, and I loved you and you didn't know it. When I crawled towards you, I just prayed, let him be alive so I can tell him, then, extraordinary as it may seem, all sorts of silly questions that only you had answers to came to mind.'

'What sort of silly questions, love?' He stroked her hand very gently so as not to hurt her cut knuckles.

'Quite irrelevant things, like why did you once meet Belinda outside the bookshop and seem so pleased to see her?'

'What?' He was obviously puzzled, and frowned.

'A while ago, one lunchtime.'

His brow cleared. 'Oh, the day I was chasing you into the bookshop and Belinda appeared. She had a crush on one of her older tutors, and wanted me to help choose him a suitable present.'

'What!' laughed Amy. 'And I thought you'd arranged to meet her, especially when you kissed and hugged so enthusiastically, and I'd been thinking you rather liked me.'

Max chuckled, then winced, as even this modest movement aggravated the bruises on his jaw. 'Rather liked you! What an understatement, my dear, sweet, silly girl. I've loved you for months, ever since that first afternoon when you were chuntering away to yourself in the treatment-room. Come closer,' he pleaded, 'and I'll prove it.'

She shuffled along the couch until their thighs touched. He cupped her chin in his hand and delicately ran the tip of his tongue along her lips in a butterfly kiss. 'I love you, Amy Kincaid,' he said firmly. 'And when we're both recovered from our battle scars, I'll demonstrate it in a much more positive way.'

Amy returned his kiss as boldly as she dared, considering her tender mouth and his bruised jaw.

The internal phone rang at that moment and the receptionist informed them that Carter had arrived to drive them home.

Max said, 'We'll have to shelve matters for the

moment. But don't forget where we were at, dear girl.'

'Oh, I won't,' said Amy. 'I promise.'

Two days later, Max and Amy went out for their delayed special meal, *à deux*.

Max had chosen the Old George Hotel at the end of Market Street, a substantial eighteenth-century hostelry with a reputation for good but plain food. He had abandoned his original idea of somewhere more exotic out of town, for several reasons.

For one thing, both he and Amy were still recovering from the events of the previous Tuesday; catching up on work that had been postponed that afternoon, and enduring interviews with the police, press and television. Life had hardly been their own since the shooting.

It had surprised them to find how emotionally as well as physically they had been affected since the shooting. They felt distressed on behalf of the family involved.

Apparently the husband was out of work and living rough. He didn't get on with his in-laws, with whom his wife and son were living. After several incidents when he had been abusive and aggressive, the court had temporarily denied him access to his son. On Tuesday he had taken the law into his own hands and tried to take his son from his wife. No one knew where he had got the gun from, or why he had gone berserk with it in the Cathedral Cloisters.

Max was still limping and walking with the aid of a stick, and Amy was still generally bruised and tender from being dragged over the paving stones. It made sense to go out for a low-key meal, and just to be together for an uninterrupted hour or so was all they wanted.

Max had booked a table tucked away behind an

elegant carved screen in the deep window embrasure.
The lighting was mellow beneath dark satin ribbed
lampshades, the cloth and napkins frosty white and the
heavy old-fashioned cutlery gleaming. It was comfortable and solid, and a far cry from the turbulent event in
which they had been involved. It was exactly right for
them at this time.

There was champagne, ice-cold in a silver bucket,
and as soon as they were seated Max signalled the
waiter to fill the two tall fluted glasses.

He leaned across and gently clinked his glass against
Amy's. 'I love you,' he said softly. 'I honestly don't
think I can add anything to that, though I'd prepared
quite a speech for what was to be a special occasion last
Tuesday. Now, after all that's happened, it seems
irrelevant. It was variations on "I love you", leading to
a sensible discussion on plans for getting married,
bearing in mind our commitments to all and sundry.
Now, my darling, all I want to add to "I love you" is,
please may we get married soon, and to hell with
everything else?'

Amy looked at him over the rim of her glass, loving
every line of his lean, still tired face, every strand of
wiry grey-black hair. His brilliant, intelligent grey eyes
looked directly into hers, and she felt she would drown
in their depths. Here was the man she loved and might
have lost two days ago. The terror of those few brief
moments when she had crawled towards his recumbent
form, not sure whether he was dead or alive, came to
her vividly.

She shivered, and her glass rattled noisily against his.
Carefully he placed his own glass on the table and
removed hers from her cold fingers. He covered her
shaking hands with his steady ones. He seemed to know
what she was thinking.

'It was terrifying, wasn't it, my love? All the while I was grappling with that chap, and afterwards when I was completely winded and the last shot had gone off, I was desperate to know that you were safe. When I heard your voice, and saw your dear, lovely face looking into mine, everything was suddenly all right, nothing else mattered. That's what suddenly rattled you, wasn't it, remembering how it feels when one's beloved is in mortal danger?'

Amy managed a smile of sorts, thinking how appropriate his old-fashioned and stylish phrase summed up her feelings. But then he was like that, her Max—precise, at times rather withdrawn, distant as some of the staff at St Anne's thought him. He wouldn't change, and she wouldn't want him to; she was prepared for the whole man. Austere but compassionate, with a dry humour and a private but loving heart. A kind man sometimes hiding behind a cool façade. A good doctor, who would be wedded as much to his profession as to her, and she loved him, and he loved her. There really wasn't anything to say except yes, to his suggestion.

'Yes,' she breathed in a whisper of a voice. 'Let's get married as soon as possible.'

Ten days later, a fortnight before Christmas, they were married in the village church, as they had both wanted.

The Rector had pulled out all the stops, and in spite of Christmas being his busiest season he had managed to find a gap in his calendar.

Max had secured a special licence so that they didn't have to have the banns called for three consecutive Sundays. By some miracle, he had arranged for most of his family, and Great-Aunt Megan, and his ex-in-laws, the Brownings, and with Belinda's help several of Amy's closest friends, to be at the wedding.

Belinda too had been responsible for organising a wedding dress and bridesmaids' dresses for herself and Rose and Jenny. To a protesting Amy, who had said that as long as she could be married in church, and to to Max, she didn't care what she wore, Belinda explained that it would be doing her friend, who had just started a boutique, a favour by having dresses from her.

Amy, for so long used to budgeting carefully, found the sum that Max had transferred to her bank account, and which he had casually instructed her to use for dresses and any odds and ends that she might need, enormous. It took all Belinda's ingenuity and guile to convince her that it was only fair to Max to put on a good show, and agree to spend what she thought of as the astronomical sums for wedding finery.

It snowed on their wedding morning, just as it had been doing on and off over the past weeks. A few fluttering flakes at intervals, settling on the frozen ground, then a great flurry as Amy and Max came out of church to a crescendo of bells ringing out joyfully. They stood in the porch for the obligatory photograph, first alone, and then with the bridesmaids, and, at Amy's insistence, a reluctant Harry.

They left the church between a column of saluting Boy Scouts, headed by a beaming Richard Dent and his mate Kevin, much to the surprise of both Amy and Max.

Confetti mixed with snowflakes as the congregation, which seemed to contain most of the villagers, followed them down the church path to the shiny Rolls-Royce that was to take them to the Manor House, the reception, and, of course, home.

4 MEDICAL ROMANCES
AND 2 FREE GIFTS
From Mills & Boon

Capture all the excitement, intrigue and emotion of the busy medical world by accepting four FREE Medical Romances, plus a FREE cuddly teddy and special mystery gift. Then if you choose, go on to enjoy 4 more exciting Medical Romances every month! Send the coupon below at once to:

MILLS & BOON READER SERVICE, FREEPOST PO BOX 236, CROYDON, SURREY CR9 9EL.

NO STAMP REQUIRED

- - -✂- -✂- - -

YES! Please rush me my 4 Free Medical Romances and 2 Free Gifts! Please also reserve me a Reader Service Subscription. If I decide to subscribe, I can look forward to receiving 4 Medical Romances every month for just £6.40, delivered direct to my door. Post and packing is free, and there's a free Mills & Boon Newsletter. If I choose not to subscribe I shall write to you within 10 days - I can keep the books and gifts whatever I decide. I can cancel or suspend my subscription at any time. I am over 18.

EP19D

Name (Mr/Mrs/Ms) _____

Address _____

_____

_____ Postcode _____

Signature _____

— MEDICAL ❤ ROMANCE —

The books for enjoyment this month are:

BEYOND HEAVEN AND EARTH Sara Burton
SISTER AT HILLSIDE Clare Lavenham
IN SAFE HANDS Margaret O'Neill
STORM IN PARADISE Judith Worthy

❤ ❤ ❤ ❤ ❤

Treats in store!

Watch next month for the following absorbing stories:

PLAYING THE JOKER Caroline Anderson
ROMANCE IN BALI Margaret Barker
SURGEON'S STRATEGY Drusilla Douglas
HEART IN JEOPARDY Patricia Robertson